INTERNET DATING
FOUR DUMMIES

A
"Luv Actually"
Escapade

By

Tony Bellino

BellStar Productions
Brisbane, Australia

INTERNET DATING FOUR DUMMIES

A "LUV ACTUALLY" ESCAPADE

Published by BellStar Productions

Copyright © Tony Bellino 2013

www.bellstarproductions.com

ISBN 10: 0-9922916-0-7
ISBN 13: 978-0-9922916-0-0

ISBN 978-0-9922916-0-0

9 780992 291600 >

Printed by CreateSpace, An Amazon.Com Company

www.amazon.com

Acknowledgements

To Mama Bear, my family, friends, and mentors
Noel & Stu, who continue to impart wisdom &
support me unconditionally; my cover artist
Gary Young: www.garycartoonist.com.au; my
editors John Jehu and Elizabeth Haris who
crossed my t's, dotted my i's, salt and peppered;
and to Joe, Sean, and Jodie, for your trust
and respect - Tonino.

DEDICATION

This book is dedicated to any committed lovers who met on a blind date, and to all puckers that gave or received their first kiss while playing "Spin The Bottle!"

God Bless Y'all.

CHAPTER I

SUB-TROPICAL cities weather three distinct summer patterns every year: ridiculously hot and humid, pissing down wet and muggy and 'Stuff this heat, we're off to the beach!' Today it was ridiculously hot and humid in Brisbane, the capital of Queensland, Australia. Even though on the world stage it's reasonably unknown, believe it or not, on a borough or a city council scale it's the third largest on the globe, behind Tokyo, with just over a million inhabitants.

Like all cities Brisney Land attracts its fair share of country folk looking for the city lifestyle, burnt out city slickers who crave genuine small city hospitality, and myriads of others in between. It holds its own when it comes to the latest gadgets, modern architecture, and equal opportunity employment. Therefore, an industrial vehicle repair floor was perhaps not the last place you'd expect to find someone with knockout curves and an irresistible smile.

Like many girls that had been raised on a farm 23 year old Nicky Kross was a master at welding, flame-cutting steel, and sandblasting—her jack-of-all-trades dad had been the perfect teacher. Not only did her job in an industrial repair shop give her a nice tradies income, but the routine of moving heavy steel in a hot environment from Monday to Friday saved her from having to tone up at crowded gyms, which was the norm for office girls.

Nicky's apprentices also knew how lucky they were to have a hot young thing as their teacher. Without fail, Neil and Bob always managed to stand extra close to her, ogling her voluptuous sweat-streaked derrière from behind as she bent extremely low to pick up fresh and dump used welding rods, over and over and over again. Knowing what she was really capable of they wouldn't have let her catch them more then once with their welding masks up and their jaws all but nailed to the floor.

Too late!

They spun around pretending to be busy but she knew their game and realised what she had to do to fuse their gobs shut once and for all. She cut the power to her welder, opened her welding mask and walked over to their workstation like a Wild West gunslinger.

'You like what you see?' Nicky questioned from about two feet behind them.

'Don't know what you're talking about,' Neil replied.

She let out a sigh of disappointment. 'Ohhh . . . that's such a shame, 'cause if you did I'd be more than happy to show you what I'm wearing under my overalls.' She looked up suggestively, batting her eyelashes for extra effect.

BINGO!

They both turned around, their eyes practically falling out of their heads.

'Really?' Bob asked incredulously.

'Sure, but first things first. Take your masks off,' she commanded. They smiled at each other and obligingly took off their masks as she continued.

'Very good! Now hold them up like this.' Nicky held her mask high above her head; Neil and Bob mirrored her action.

Next, she undid the top two buttons of her overalls and cupped them to her breasts before they fell. She paused for effect. 'You ready?' she asked.

'Shit yeah!' they panted in unison.

Nicky paused a moment longer then ripped her overalls open in a fluid downward motion revealing her favourite t-shirt: Bruce Lee in a Kung-Fu pose from the movie "Enter The Dragon." As the boys stared, hypnotised to the potent image on her chest, she let rip.

'KEE-YAH!'

Nicky front-kicked the mask above Neil's head sending it spinning backwards that landed 10 metres away with a loud thud. In another fluid motion she spun around and roundhouse kicked the other mask out of Bob's grip with a piercing,

'HA-CHE!'

That saw it skitter backward and rocket under the 10 tonne grader she'd just been working on. She jumped toward the boys who were still in shock. '

BOO!'

Bob flinched, reflexively putting his hands over his head in protection, which made Nicky piss herself laughing. She victory danced back to the ladies' locker room, without wasting so much as another glance at the losers behind her.

Nicky opened her locker and stripped off before folding a towel over her shoulders in preparation for a shower. The sight of her tattoo in the mirror forced her to stop. She fingered the small boxing kangaroo inked just under her bikini line on her right hip as she remembered the night she had gotten it done, as well as her first boyfriend Jason who had an identical tattoo to match. *The things we do when we're in love*, she thought, *but is there ever a more consuming ardour?*

Her parents had loved and approved of Jason but in a town of only 400 people it was hard to avoid running into him once they had split up, so she decided to move to the big smoke. However, she was damn sure neither her mum nor her dad would approve of her current love interest.

CHAPTER II

FOR young teen Alex Trainer coming home from school to an empty house was both the sweetest and most sour part of her day. Sweet because she got to turn her stereo way up for an hour or so before her dad arrived home. Sour because, although inspired to learn how to cook from her mum's favourite TV show Junior Master Chef, her mother's passing away a year earlier from cancer often made dinner preparation a time for sad reflection.

Hanging over the dividing fence and waiting for Alex as she came up the drive was over fifty-something neighbour, Sally. Alex knew exactly why she was smiling at her like a Cheshire Cat and for whom she had baked the freshly creamed chocolate cake that she held in her hands. *And* why she was wearing a skirt the size of Alex's belt: but her Dad was nowhere in sight.

Alex's dad, John, was 5'9 and all muscle. Somehow he'd managed to keep his fitness in check despite the anguish of the past twelve months. Her late mum, Grace, had passed on her rare genes to her daughter, leaving her with chestnut coloured hair, clear blue eyes and a feisty temper. A temper that seemed to always flare when Sally was around.

'Hi, missy, how was school?' Sally asked.

'Same ol', same ol'…want to listen to some music?' Alex asked.

'Maybe later,' was Sally's melancholy reply.

'Yeah, when my dad's home,' Alex muttered under her breath. She pointed to the cake.

'Is that for me?'

'And your dad too,' was Sally's fast reply. Alex accepted the cake like a smiling assassin.

'You know he's not interested in you.' Alex smiled contentedly as she witnessed Sally's face fall ever so slightly.

'That's not why I made it,' Sally replied, a tad insecurely.

That was all Alex needed.

'Yes it is,' Alex corrected. 'But you should know — he's just not interested in shagging a cougar!'

The look Alex left on Sally's face somewhat resembled a mechanical Ping-Pong ball-swallowing clown. As she made her way up the stairs and through the back door with a smile on her dial and a freshly baked chocolate cake in her hands she headed straight for the bin where she dumped the cake as though it carried the plague. She proceeded to switch on the air conditioning and finally turn on her dad's Dynamic surround-sound stereo system winding the volume up as high as would not get any complaints from the neighbours. She bopped all the way to the kitchen as though she were in a music video, immersing herself within the pounding beat as she deftly timed each dance move with the action of reaching for an ingredient for tonight's dinner.

The next part of her routine was to tie her hair into a ponytail; she always wore it over her cheeks like a hood when out of the house. In fact, dinner preparation was the only time of the day you could look upon her whole face. She unsheathed her favourite knife, opened her Thai cookbook to page 12 and began chop-chopping vegies to the rhythm blaring from the stereo. On a visit to the sink she looked out the window and noticed Sally pacing up and down on her veranda with her phone glued to her ear.

*****

What made John a good dad was also what had made him a great husband. It simply came down to being a caring friend who always listened. The issue preoccupying him on the peak hour drive home from the office tonight was the call he'd received from an irate and insulted Sally. He thought about how he was going to delicately deal with Alex and her earlier confrontation with Sally. While calling Sally a cougar did amuse him he was more concerned with where the heck his 13-year-old had picked up the slang word "shagging"? He decided to add Austin Powers' name to his "To Punch" list.

He recognised the aroma as soon as he walked through the front door: stir-fried hokkien noodles with bok choy and hoisin sauce. Grace's favourite. It was a sign that Alex was missing her mum a little bit extra tonight so he expected the rest of the evening to consist of either a relaxed dinner together, or a very short fight with his feisty daughter and dinner on the couch. It was that simple.

At first sight Alex ran into his arms and kissed him on his chin as she always did.

'Hi Daddy, are you hungry?'

'Hello Cupcake. I'm famished.'

'Take a seat.' Alex pulled out a chair for him like a maître d'. 'How was your day?' she asked, before making a move to the hot wok on the stove.

He glanced around and his initial suspicions were confirmed when he saw the framed picture of Grace in front of one of the place settings on the dining table. He said a silent prayer for wisdom as he sat down and then waited for Alex to return with their dinner.

'Alex, I know mum's passing is still affecting you but have you considered that every time I look at you I see her?' John looked at the photo of his wife and then back to Alex with a raised eyebrow.

'No you don't!' she retorted, raising her voice slightly.

'How's Sally?' he questioned as she began to serve the noodles.

'Sally from school?'

'No, Sally from next door,' he affirmed.

'Don't know, haven't seen her,' she fibbed.

'So what's for dessert?' he probed.

'Banana-split ice cream.'

'No cake? Chocolate cake, to be precise?' he queried.

Alex looked him straight back in the eye and shook her head

'No.'

John got up, walked to the bin and put a foot on the pedal.

'NO DADDY!' Alex cried out.

'What's to hide if we're having banana-split ice cream?' He brought his foot down, opening the bin.

'You and Sally tricked me!' Alex yelled, her voice filling with emotion.

'Why would we do that?'

'Because. . .' she paused. 'I hate you.'

As if he'd not heard that before.

'No you don't, sweetie, but just because Sal and I talk from time to time it doesn't mean . . . she's just a friend, OK?"

Alex knew that lying was her dad's number one pet hate so she decided to play the sympathy/self-pity card before the end of the rally.

'What about me? Do you care about me?' she started to tear up, despite herself.

'That's exactly what this is all about.' he countered, exasperated.

'No it's not, it's all about you and Sally making ME look stupid.'

John felt her desperation and decided not to argue the point. Besides, he was just too tired to keep it up.

'Alex you're all I have! I know your needs come first, but if I'm going to include someone else in our lives she'll have to be right for the both of us.

But that'll all take time, not luck, and definitely not the cougar next door.'

Alex took a second to process and then they both laughed at his use of the word cougar.

'I'm sorry, dad. What can I do to help?' she said, putting a hand on his shoulder.

He smiled sadly. If only she knew how unmotivated he was feeling in regards to pursuing a new relationship she would be over the moon. Of course he had his moments of loneliness, like all virile mid-thirties men, but he was only just recently finding women attractive again.

'Be patient, be yourself and it will all fall into place for the both of us,' he assured her.

Alex stared at her mum's photo as he hugged her.

'I wonder if mummy has a twin?' she said over his shoulder to herself.

'What's that?' he asked.

Alex leaned back and looked him straight in the eyes.

'Sorry about the cake in the bin.'

John kissed her gently on the forehead.

'Who needs cake, my darling, when I have you!'

CHAPTER III

PROFESSOR Lorrie Chester, or just Chester as he preferred to be called, used the afternoon country drive to pick up his wife Laura to sort out his daily stressors. He'd been an educator since graduating in 1963 and a university dean for twenty years but the last decade, due to Laura's wheel-chair binding affliction, had been his most trying one yet.

Being a man of conservative values he, in his own opinion, only had one obvious vice — driving his speedy vintage convertible red MG every weekend; but he hadn't driven it in 10 years. Sadly, it had been replaced by a van, a disabled transporter to cater for Laura's wheelchair. This drive through the countryside often reminded him of the journeys they used to take together in their antique red rocket.

Yet more than this Chester missed Laura's carefree laugh, the generous smile that used to grace her lips and especially her unconditional love. These had all withered away along with every hope she'd had of ever walking again. Now he truly didn't recognise the person she'd become; even her pretty face was slowly being eroded away by the passing time and never-ending torment she seemed to endure.

As he pulled-up next to the show jumping practice paddock he noticed that Laura's final student for the day was 16 year old Penny, Laura's most awarded and successful pupil. In the two years she'd been Laura's student Penny had gone from being an OK jumper to a state contender, but something was still blocking her full potential. Chester's years of teaching had identified the problem but the wall Laura had put up between them constantly stopped her from receiving his expert advice.

'NO, NO, NO!' Laura yelled at the top of her lungs as Penny knocked off the last rung of a triple hurdle combination.

'Sorry, Mrs Chester,' Penny said with a sad disposition. 'He stalls at that hurdle every time.'

'Well it's your job to get him up and over it every time,' Laura retorted without empathy. Having noticed Chester's arrival she decided that was it for today.

'Enough! Make sure he's as clean as a whistle before you stall him.'

'Yes, Mrs Chester.'

'You're way too hard on her you know,' Chester commented as Laura wheeled past him.

'In forty years have I ever advised you on how to educate any of your students?' she said, effectively ending the discussion.

As he made the short walk to the driver's door he knew that any attempt to help her in through the rear elevator door would invite venomous comments about his lack of acknowledging her self-sufficiency. He sat in the driver's seat avoiding any eye contact with her via the rear-vision mirror and waiting until he heard the seatbelt buckle click before he started the engine. It was going to be an uncomfortably long and quiet trip back home.

CHAPTER IV

HER newspaper ad was a masterpiece. It read:

AAA: Luxury penthouse room for rent. Single 20-something female seeks a male flatmate. Fully furnished, pool, spa, sauna, car space, inner city. $140 per week all bills inclusive. Phone Rene after 8am on 0559 384 291.

Writing the ad was the easy part. What worried Rene were two things: she wasn't exactly a twenty-something female (on her next birthday she'd turn thirty five), and she wasn't exactly the type of girl you'd expect living in a penthouse in the city, what with the eighteen plus kilos she'd unintentionally added to her 5'8 frame since arriving in Australia three months ago from South Africa. There was, however, a glorious bonus to this weight gain, for she was now a buxom 12D as opposed to her usual size of 8C. Rene had decided to disclose her age to potential flat mates only if she was asked about it outright—there was no point in turning off a cute boy before he'd even seen the apartment, now, was there!

She'd started sorting out the men from the boys from 8.05am and had three acceptable candidates by 8.25am. The forth call of the morning was from husky-voiced Jake.

'Is the room still available?' he asked.

'Indeed.' she answered, smiling through the phone.

'What time you open for inspections?'

Straight to the point. She liked him already! She gave him the next available time slot and then hung up, already starting to fantasise about what he looked like. She then began to prepare for their arrivals. The first entry of the day was 24-

year-old barista Sebastian scheduled for 10am on the dot. As she applied her make-up she continued fantasising about having a man in her life again, even if it was, on this occasion, by deceptive housemate proxy.

Jake rang Rene's doorbell 45 minutes early. He had too been fantasizing about the apartment since he had spoken to Rene that morning and couldn't wait to see the place. He had already started planning future summer pool parties and Saturday night TV football nights with his mates; and with a base so central to city pubs and clubs he smiled at the thought of all the money he'd save on taxis by bringing girls home on foot. He couldn't wait to see what $140 a week was going to get him and arrived eager to quash the feeling that Rene's ad was really too good to be true.

'Top floor, first door on the left,' Rene spoke into the intercom, but something in her voice suggested she wasn't happy he was early. As he opened the foyer door, Jake was bowled over by a scrambling Sebastian, running and screaming past him at top speed. He shrugged his shoulders wondering what the fuss was about and continued on his way to paradise.

Jake found the apartment with ease and after he had knocked on the door started to wish he had not put on so much cologne—he was getting nauseous just standing there smelling himself. He looked up and smiled in preparation as the door began to open…and then he wished he'd never laid eyes on her or her ad!

'Hi Jake, I'm Rene. Come in.' She stood aside to let him in.

'Please, after you.' he gestured.

As Rene turned around his jaw dropped to the floor. Of the extra weight Rene had put on, and after excluding the 4kg sitting on her chest 14 had found a home on her hips and buttocks! His mind instantly took a suicidal trip down memory lane when his mum had made a giant raspberry jelly and fruit tower for his birthday. It seemed to take on a life of its own as it careered insanely up and down and side to side as she carried it into the dining room. He watched Rene waddling away in front of him—up and down and side to side, just like that jelly—and ran.

Rene stopped and closed her eyes in pain and shame as she heard the door slam. *Surely Australian men can't all be this shallow*, she thought to herself as she sank to the floor, huge tears welling in her eyes. She had to talk to someone before the next contender arrived, and there was only one person in the whole country she trusted with such personal matters: her mum.

'Give it a little more time,' Rene's mum, Kara, told her. Rene who had been weeping from the outset of the call was now calming down. 'We know how beautiful you are on the inside,' Kara reassured her.

Rene's door buzzer interrupted their heart-to-heart.

'Thanks mum, but I have to go. Someone's at the door.' Rene took in the vision on the intercom screen and it took her breath away. She stood there for five long seconds before picking up the hand piece. 'Can I help you?' she asked, assuming this gorgeous man was lost.

'I'm here to see the room,' he stated, effeminately.

'It's been take—' Rene cut her reply short and quickly reset her attitude. 'Top floor, first door on the left.'

Rene rushed to the mirror, adjusted herself and wiped the watered-down mascara tracks off her cheeks. She took a deep breath and went to open the door. Standing before her was a man with a face that many would say was 'too beautiful' for a male and not a gram of fat could be found anywhere on his body. Yet neither of these were the reasons Rene was left searching for breath. Rather, it was the Pink Panther coloured tracksuit he was wearing, unzipped just far enough to get an eyeful of his clean skin six pack.

'I'm Derrick, and you must be Rene, yes?' Before she could respond he added, 'Oh my gosh, look at that view!' He pushed past her into the hall, through the dining room and onto the veranda at break-neck speed.

She caught up with him, slightly short of breath, and took in the gorgeous view of the city from her apartment,

'Now this is what I came here for!' he exclaimed. Like greased lightning he switched his interest back to the inside of the apartment and zipped past her into the dining room. Rene also did an about face and joined him as he studied a family portrait on the wall.

'What a beautiful family you have…and your brothers, so cute!' Once again before she could comment he skittered into the kitchen and opened her stainless steel fridge door. 'Hmmm…lots of little naughties in here, but we can work our way through them as we go.'

The fridge door was still closing as he took off again, this time into the lounge room.

'Yum, yum! Seventy-two inches of pure, Blu-ray delight-a-vision!' he squealed. He stroked a finger over the frame checking for dust and then turned, pointing to the closed door nearby. 'Is that my boudoir?' he questioned, raising his eyebrows a few times and smiling cheekily.

Unable to speak, Rene just nodded. Like a child making his way to the presents under a Christmas tree, Derrick tiptoed to the door and opened it ever so slowly.

'Agggggrrrrrrhhhhhhhhh!' he screamed, and then slammed it shut.

'What's the matter?' Rene questioned, shocked.

'That bedspread — it's ghastly! I'm sorry but I have to leave.' Derrick tried to push past her, first to the right then to the left, but Rene's wide, double-bubble helped her hold her ground.

'I can buy a new bedspread,' she pleaded. 'With matching curtains,' she added quickly.

'It…it's not really the bedspread.' Derrick broke down, sobbing. 'I just can't afford the rent!'

'Even at a hundred & forty doll —'

'He took everything! My whole life savings! I just had to move away.' He stopped, looking at Rene like a lost puppy. 'You understand don't you?'

'What? Who?' Rene was now confused.

'My ex-partner! We opened a personal training studio together in Sydney. I didn't read all the fine print on the lease and then one day — BAM — he just walked out the door!'

Rene burst into tears.

'Don't worry sweetie, I'll be fine. Eventually.' He put an arm around her shoulders.

'You don't understand,' Rene exclaimed. 'My fiancée promised we'd move here together, get married and start a family.' She sniffed, not worrying about what she looked like anymore. 'Then, a week before we were booked to leave South Africa, he broke it off. VIA SMS!'

'My, my…you poor dear.' He continued to hold her close.

'All I've done since arriving here is watch chick flicks, eat junk food and cry myself to sleep. I have nobody here Derrick nobody. Look!'

Rene pointed to an old picture of herself hanging on the wall. He stared at it in disbelief. *Could this be the same person?*

'Oh my God! You were a Babelicious Princess!'

As Derrick hugged her, he could feel warm tears starting to soak through his pink tracksuit top but as suddenly as she started, she stopped crying and pulled away from him.

'Wait, I have an idea! Perhaps we can help each other?'

Derrick wasn't sure where this was heading.

'What do you mean?'

'What if you stay here and personally train me back into a Babelicious Princess, and in return I'll waive three months rent?' Rene held out her hand. 'Deal?' she coaxed.

'Singed and sealed, Sugar Pie.' Derrick couldn't stop grinning, thinking he'd just made the deal of the century.

What he didn't know, however, was that Rene had paid cash for this penthouse from the profits she had made after selling her businesses back in South Africa, and it was still continuing to increase in value every month. She didn't really need the money. She was just waiting for the depression of her break-up to pass and the inspiration of a new business to replace it. Derrick had no idea that he was standing in the presence of an extremely savvy and very ferocious businesswoman.

And be sure that I will get my daily pound of flesh out of you, echoed in Rene's mind as Derrick squeezed her outstretched hand to seal their mutually beneficial agreement.

CHAPTER V

THREE MONTHS LATER

WHEN it came to weight loss Derrick was an expert. He'd thrown everything he had at Rene which, when combined with her tunnel vision and determination, meant she'd become an expert too.

When she first entered the weights room at the gym Rene was shy and disorientated; now she could size-up another freshman and compute an ideal resistance-training regime for them in less than 10 minutes. She was also leg pressing over four times her body weight, earning her the gym nickname 'Hot Foxed Buns'.

In her Zumba fitness class, due to the brilliant rhythm attained from childhood jazz and ballet classes, she'd become an assistant instructor and had to beat Enrique, her touchy Brazilian teacher, off with a stick. Her fridge and pantry were snapshots of the perfect dietary requirements for a high performance athlete, plus she'd learnt to blend and juice more efficiently than an infomercial model. Babelicious Princess, Babe Again Virgin, and Hot Foxed Buns all now applied to this finely tuned, supremely confident head turning machine.

There were also a few extra bonuses she'd gained in the process. Due to her rapid progress these past few months, Derrick had picked up a handful of high profile, deep-pocketed personal training clients that allowed him to recover his self-esteem and to easily pay his rent. She'd gained a best friend out of her housemate leading to great harmony and unity at home, which in turn helped her to both forgive her ex-fiancé and to release her soul from the depression she had been feeling.

However, the opportunity to display her ultimate girl-power and revenge came at the most unexpected time and place. One night at a bar not far from their apartment, she,

Derrick and two gym buddies were snuggled in a booth sharing tapas and a bottle of Sav Blanc. Looking around the bar, which was quickly filling with people, she froze. Derrick noticed her stiffen.

'What's up, Sugar Pie?'

Rene couldn't believe her luck and kept an eye on the person she'd spotted while answering Derrick.

'Nothing. I'll be back in a moment.'

She approached the bar. Standing there, all by his lonesome self was none other than about face Snake Jake. Rene crept up behind him and tapped him on the shoulder, forcing him to look the wrong way as she placed herself calmly on the bar stool on the other side of him. As he turned she saw his eyes widen in appreciation.

'Hello Jake.'

'Ha…Her…Have we met before?' he managed to stammer.

Rene stood upright, pushing her chest out.

'Tell me, Jake, are you a fun bags?' she asked as he checked her healthy puppies out.

When his eyes finally reached hers she placed an arm on the bar, bent over slightly, arched her back and flung her jacket to one side revealing her hot foxed buns. Jake took a nervous swig of his drink.

'Or are you a booty man?'

At this he sprayed his mouthful of beer into the air.

'Shame I'm out of your league, mate,' she said sarcastically, ''cause as you can see, I got both!

She laughed at the expression on his face and sexily swaggered back to join her friends, with enough adrenaline thumping through her veins to revive a fossilised T-Rex.

CHAPTER VI

BRISBANE'S Robinson College lies at the forefront of private Australian universities for two reasons: peerless lectures and first-class facilities. Its reputation ensured its students formed a diverse and eclectic mix of home grown as well as foreign protégés from the four corners of the globe; but there was always an exception to the rule.

Exactly how Will Jackson had qualified to be in the midst of these top students was a topic of much speculation. Sporting longhair and coke-bottle glasses, he was about as receptive to advanced ideas as a koala stoned on spiked eucalyptus leaves. He was currently on his second attempt at a BA majoring in business marketing at the over-ripe age of 23.

On the other hand, 28-year-old visa student Ravi Ali was on the opposite side of the spectrum. His biggest challenge came from dealing with jealous IT geeks who were 10 years his junior but only had half his natural computing ability. What had delayed Ravi's entrance into university was that it had taken his impoverished family a decade to collectively scrimp up enough funds to send him to Australia and to support him while he was there. Thus, anything less than being an honours student was incomprehensible.

The biggest question on everyone's minds today, however, was why the business marketing and the IT students were being called to assemble together. As approximately 100 students buzzed towards the Robinson Memorial theatre they filed into their seats and noticed two ballot boxes standing opposite each other on either side of a long table.

Standing behind the table were their two lecturers. Trish Bain had been the head of the IT faculty at Robinson College for four years. She was a youthful forty-something woman and very popular with her pupils due to her understanding of their large workloads and competing deadlines.

She was also a perfectionist and if she granted you an extension on a paper it had to be a masterful, worthy effort or one would be hard pressed getting another extension so easily.

Standing next to her also watching his students file in was the marketing faculty's Professor James Rosenthal, who'd been head hunted by Robinson College from a distinguished English University a few years ago. This job was his retirement package in the sun and he often counted the weeks and months until holiday time so he could take his wife on sailing trips to various parts of the continent. This combined faculty experiment was his idea, but in the back of his mind he pitied whoever had the misfortune to be partnered with his most underachieving pupil, Will Jackson.

'I'm sure you're all wondering why the marketing majors have been joined with the IT majors.' The students quieted down when Trish Bain's announcement filled the auditorium. 'To those students of mine who are not familiar with the man standing beside me, I would like to introduce the head of the marketing faculty, Professor James Rosenthal.'

After clearing his throat, Rosenthal took over.

'As you're all aware, the teaching staff here at Robinson College pride themselves on providing a rather more practical approach to the educational process. Therefore it's applicable that your final examination for the year should fully reflect this culture.'

Rosenthal's students knew what to expect next and he confirmed it by sliding a giant whiteboard down and unveiling their hand written assignment on the board behind it. He highlighted sections of it with a laser pointer.

'Every marketing student will be paired with an IT student. Each hybrid partnership will then have exactly four weeks to build, upload and market a fully functional website. The objective of the project is for each team's site to receive 1,000 cookie hits — this will be how you will receive a passing grade.'

'Easy — Porn!' called someone from the back, and sending the theatre into fits of laughter. The comedic commentator was none other than Ryan Davis, who was both the top dog of the Alpha Fraternity and Ravi Ali's chief nemesis. Though he tried to disguise his voice it was still recognisable to Trish Bain.

'Final class honours are at stake here, Mr. Davis, so there will be no porn sites,' Trish Bain emphasised. 'However, there will be practical, polished and commercially savvy ones without exception.'

'We expect and accept many of your campus classmates to view your work,' Rosenthal continued. 'However, we will be reviewing your cookies and if there are more than four from the same source — equating to 25% of your cookie trail total — then you will either fail or have the option to come back and do it all again during Summer School!'

At that the students let out a moan of protest that would have made a herd of moose proud. Bain and Rosenthal then began the task of joining their classes together by drawing out names from the boxes on the desk. One of the first teams called was Ryan Davis and geek centrefold Jane Summers.

Lucky bastard, Will thought to himself as they walked out of the auditorium door together, smiling, giggling and with Ryan's hand already affixed to the small of Jane's back. After 10 minutes the last partnership was announced.

'Ravi Muhammad Ali,' called Trish Bain.

Rosenthal hesitated, prolonging the inevitable.

'William Jackson,' he finally said, glancing at Ravi apologetically.

Will got to the front of the auditorium before Ravi and with disappointment written on his face he put a hand into Bain's box to see if Ravi's name was truly the last one left.

'Don't be so disappointed, Mr. Jackson. Ravi has been the top of his class three years running,' Trish Bain said as Ravi came to stand beside his new partner.

'I'll try to remember that,' Will retorted, before acknowledging Ravi's presence. 'Come on, Slugger!'

Not completely understanding, Ravi politely corrected him.

'Excuse me, please, but my name is Ravi, not Slugger.'

'I know. I was playing on your last two names, you know, Muhammad Ali.' Will did a one-two punch into the air trying to imitate the greatest heavy weight boxer of all time. Ravi was still clueless.

'I don't see how ones country of birth has anything to do with being called a Slugger.'

Will simply shook his head and started to leave.

'Come on Punchy, we got work to do.'

As Will exited the auditorium he left Rosenthal rolling his eyes in disbelief at his nonsense and Trish Bain shaking her head at such juvenile antics. The clueless Ravi simply followed Will outside still trying hard to work out why he wouldn't call him by his real name.

CHAPTER VII

THE news of Will and Ravi's partnering preceded them and was already a minor topic of conversation between some of the students who'd decided to get to know each other and begin the planning of their assignments at Robinson's most popular café. However, it was a major issue in the mind of Ryan Davis and he planned the launch of his verbal ambush from a table on the edge of the café as Will and Ravi approached to take a seat.

'Let's see now, who's going to be the giver and who's going to be the taker in this partnership?' Ryan smirked, evoking attention and giggles from the students on the tables either side of the one at which he was sitting.

'Sorry you got the short straw,' Will said, looking apologetically at Jane. He knew he had the better business partner and wasn't afraid to say it. Yet what Will wasn't aware of was that Jane had already chosen the outfit and underwear she was going to wear for her first date with Ryan; perhaps then he would have maturely ignored the next taunt.

'I wouldn't open my lollypop, sucker, if I were you, especially now you're joined at the hip with Mr Sun-Burned Ali!' This again amused Ryan's audience.

'Isn't Ravi top of your class?' returned Will, aiming where it hurt. 'Care to put a wager on whose team gets primo class honours?'

This made Ravi cringe. He knew exactly how much power this cashed-up, leader of the pack

Alpha Male had on their fellow students and it was his 'Achilles heel of reciprocated jealousy' for this spoilt little brat that often made him dislike his own social status.

'Ha, you two couldn't afford the service on my Mercedes, watch and learn lame brains,' Ryan replied, before he stood on his seat and with all the skill of a weathered politician began his campaign. 'Listen up everyone. You're all invited to a free beer party at Alpha dorm tonight!'

The howling roar of approval from the café crowd was so loud it gained the attention of people from nearby buildings.

'That's right. Alpha knows your needs and wants but while the beer is free entry is strictly via a hand written note that reads "I promise you that I will willfully log onto Ryan Davis and Miss Jane's web assignment and not onto that of Salt and Pepper's!"'

The crowd traced Ryan's pointing finger in unison as a stunned Will and an infuriated Ravi looked on. After an even louder roar their crescendo reached a hypnotic, 'ALPHA! ALPHA! ALPHA!'

As Ryan stood down, Ravi couldn't contain himself.

'You're a very stupid individual, Mr. Davis, and I am going to take great pleasure in seeing our website leaving yours in the dust!' Ravi exclaimed over the chant.

'Bring it on, Bozo,' Ryan chuckled, as the chant he had incited gained momentum.

As Will and Ravi began their retreat from the café, Will scribbled onto a piece of paper then handed it to his new partner in crime.

'My address and number. 7pm sharp. And Slugger, bring your A-game.' Will turned and walked away without waiting for a reply.

Observing the whole contest from his first floor office window was none other than the dean of Robinson University, Mr. Chester, whom, oblivious to the contents of the verbal duel, was filled with pride by the loud chants for his most renowned and popular fraternity. He let the curtains fall then turned to his new secretary.

'You hear that Miss Green?'

'Yes, Mr. Chester,' she replied.

'That's the sacred echo of Robinson College unity, our students finest quality. In time you too will see your work here as one of the greatest achievements of your professional working life.' As Chester strolled back to his antique oak desk he habitually picked up a youthful picture of Laura and stared deep into it, temporally forgetting Miss Green's presence.

'Is that your wife?' she asked, breaking the silence.

'We were childhood sweethearts, you know,' Chester stated proudly.

'She's very beautiful,' Miss Green said, admiring the photo.

'That will be all for now,' said Chester, ending the moment and replacing the picture on his desk.

As Miss Green closed the door behind her Chester retrieved his rosary beads from his pocket. He began to recite a prayer in hope it would again quell the stabbing pain that always consumed him when he dwelt on Laura's immobilising disability.

CHAPTER VIII

DEAD on 7pm, Ravi found himself ascending the stairs of Will's student apartment block with a pile of books and his trusty laptop in his grasp. He'd spent most of his afternoon firstly contemplating the events of the morning's confrontation with Ryan and secondly, trying to work out how he was going to pitch his assignment idea to his new partner. The strategy he'd selected was like Will, quite simple really: *Lead a horse to water and don't let it stop drinking till it's drowned!* he thought, and then laughed out loud, despite himself. Besides, he'd already booked and paid for his end of semester vacation and he was not letting anything, especially the threat of summer school, knock him off his holiday cloud.

At the same time as Ravi was about to knock on his door Will was spying out of his lounge room window through a pair of binoculars. Like a racetrack commentator, he was giving a running commentary to his flatmate, Abigail, of the arrivals and party events happening in the top floor apartment of the next building, the home of the Alpha fraternity. He wished he was mixing it up in there himself until he remembered it was being thrown in his and Ravi's honour, or more precisely, their dishonour. Shit, for a night of free beer he was happy to let his pride take a battering and go in disguise. He only came to his senses when he heard the knock on his door. He closed the curtain and hid his binoculars before answering.

'Come in Slugger,' he said, waving Ravi in.

'Thank you very much,' Ravi politely replied. He entered Will's apartment and plonked his books and laptop on the study table. He stared at the glass enclosure where Will's pet tarantula lived: it took pride of place in Will's lounge room where the TV would normally sit.

'Don't get too close to her. I've tried and she doesn't like Indian,' Will warned Ravi, trying to make a joke.

'Suits me fine, I'm actually from Pakistan,' Ravi corrected.

Had Will known the political and religious difference, it would have been comical.

'OK...Ah...Well,' Will stammered, clearly confused, 'I've come up with this.' He handed Ravi a mess of disordered, handwritten notes.

'What's this?' Ravi questioned, trying to figure out the last page from the first.

'Money Free Dot Com,' Will said proudly, before launching into his pitch. 'Here's how it plays. We offer a site where consumers can get things for free, like just out of date tinned food, cool stuff from industrial bins, and department store dumpsters where they throw out slightly damaged goods. Thoughts?'

Since Ravi was a gentleman, he couldn't convey his real thoughts, so he took a moment to compose himself.

'I think you should remember who is the IT specialist and who is responsible for the marketing!' Ravi exclaimed, rather loudly.

'We're in this together, what's the harm if I help out?' Will replied, his own voice also becoming raised.

'OK, then, let's explore your theory,' Ravi retorted, now a little more calm. 'How long will it take to find these venues we would get stuff from, give or take?'

'A week or two,' Will answered, as if it wouldn't be a problem.

'How long to get pictures, maps, approvals, testimonials from customers and the like?' Ravi continued to probe.

Will tried to look intelligent as he thought about the answer. Finally, he shrugged.

'About the same.'

Ravi couldn't believe Will didn't see where all this was leading in regards to the assignment's one-month restriction for completion, so he let him have the full picture.

'What about building the web pages, writing and testing the software code, uploading the site, ironing out teething problems, and the marketing of it all—off campus and direct to the public thanks to your unfriendly wager with Mr. Davis?'

Will's comeback was again a blank shrug. Ravi held up Will's notes.

'Add this all up in weeks and we will be in summer school before we begin. And I have better things to do on my vacation!'

'Why are you so negative, man?' Will asked.

'Permission to review my idea?' Ravi ignored Will's inane question and proceeded to show him his own. He opened his laptop on the table, tapped the keyboard, and then swivelled it around for Will to peruse.

'Love Inc Dot Com...is this porn? You heard Miss —'

'IT IS NOT PORN! However, it is perhaps the most refined dating site of its kind in Australia today!'

'Where did you get all the photos of these girls from? Man she's cute!' Will kept on nodding in appreciation as he clicked through the site.

Not amused nor flattered, Ravi continued.

'Now click onto the member benefits page, please.'

Will did as directed then began to read from the screen.

'Ten free babysitting vouchers for single parents! 50% discounts at selected restaurants and cinemas! Free marriage counselling! Free condoms! 30-day money back guarantee if not 100% satisfied!' He turned to Ravi. 'Weren't you just lecturing me about getting approvals from —'

Once again, Ravi cut him off 'that's all irrelevant! Click onto the membership page, please.'

Will let out a sigh, opened then began to read the page.

'FIVE HUNDRED BUCKS! You're crazy man!'

Ravi couldn't believe the depths of Will's ignorance. Here, in front of his eyes and at his fingertips, was a complete and functioning website that needed nothing other than Will's approval for weeks of student sweat and toil to be bypassed, yet all this dingbat could do was critique minor details? Truth be told, the driving force behind the three long months that it had taken Ravi to compile, code, and test his masterpiece had been this scene, the very unveiling of his prized jewel to his partner, the elation and joy it should and in fact would bring to the team. Instead, he got this? Blah, blah, blah from a Garth Alger clone who had a spider for a housemate!

'You're missing the whole point!' Ravi exclaimed.

'Which is?' Will asked.

'We don't really want anyone to join the site, nor do we want to operate such an enormous concern, but with such benefits as these we've a site worthy to exploit the desperate singles market and to get our one thousand cookie hits, yes?'

'Maybe,' Will said.

'And since it's ready to upload, all we have to concentrate on is the marketing and advertising, correct?' Ravi pressed on, hopeful Will would come to his senses. And then finally — an intelligent question! However, it was the only one Ravi had hoped he wouldn't ask.

'Ravi, how did you know to build this site before we even got the assignment in class today?'

Ravi had already prepared an answer, but one he was not ready to give away just yet.

'I'll answer your query if you grant me a small favour,' Ravi punted.

Which is?' Will asked, intrigued.

Ravi slid the pile of thick textbooks he'd brought with him across the table to sit in front of Will.

'These books contain the greatest marketing and branding secrets known to modern mankind. I've personally marked my favourites for you to choose from. As soon as you confirm those to kick-off our enterprise I'll let you in on my little secret!' he said.

After a few moments they finally had a deal that was confirmed when Will extended his hand to Ravi, who joyfully accepted it.

'I'm so looking forward to showing Mr. Davis who the real Bozo is!' Ravi smiled at Will who grinned back in return.

'Me too, Slugger, me too!'

CHAPTER IX

NICKY'S karate Dojo was a converted community hall located on the outer suburbs of Brisbane city. It catered for many family units that trained together and she often had trouble finding a car park but tonight it was a breeze for she had been called in half an hour early by her Sensei Kate, a former national karate champion herself. Strangely, however, she had not called her in to train. As their training groups arrived and began their warm-ups and kata, Nicky and Kate were off in a dark side office, seated together on a couch watching a home movie. The film had two stars: Nicky, and her sporting nemesis from New South Wales, Olivia Carter, who had beaten her in the national karate final the last three years. The film they were watching was their most recent contest.

'You see right there!' Kate pointed to the screen referring to a counter move Olivia had used against one of Nicky's offensive kicks. This move had given Olivia the vital position in setting up the move that gave her the championship. Nicky could barely watch it, even now.

'See how she moves with the momentum, that was your best front kick!' Kate's comment was so confronting.

'Lucky bitch,' Nicky snarled.

'There's no luck in karate, kid. She simply knows your style and that's why she's the Australian champion!'

Nicky's blood started to boil.

'So what do I do, change everything I've ever learned?' she hissed.

Kate stood up and paced the floor in front of the screen.

'The finals are less than a month away, so you don't have time to do that,' Kate said as a matter-of-fact.

'So?' Nicky asked.

As the video continued streaming over Kate's torso she had a Eureka! moment.

'You have to trick her. Confuse her, so she doesn't know what's coming.'

'But how?' asked Nicky.

'Well…in the first phase, fake every second or third kick, like a kickboxer!

Kate demonstrated the technique with both legs, hopping from one foot to the other and pretending to kick Nicky. 'Then, in the second phase, you fake every kick. But, by the third phase, she won't know whether you're faking or whether you're for real! She'll never see what's coming!' Kate smiled at her own trickery.

'Which is?' Nicky was still unsure where Kate was going with this.

'She's beaten you three times IN A ROW and you've never ever dreamed it? Then you deserve second best!' Kate shouted.

Surprised at the anger of her mentor Nicky sprang to her feet like a cat and attacked Kate unexpectedly, simulating a Kato vs. Inspector Clouseau scene from the movie The Pink Panther.

Kate then showed Nicky why she was her Sensei as well as the dominant partner in their love affair by pinning her to the wall with a side-stepping move and a twist.

'That's my feisty girl. Now, here's what you do. Spar with every kickboxer you can find, male or female, from now until the finals.'

'But I don't know any…' Nicky hesitated.

Wanting to release her from her grip asap but also wanting to highlight her point, Kate didn't let her finish.

'Three rounds, exactly as I say. Then, like magic, your subconscious will answer you. Trust me!'

Nicky stopped her struggle and relaxed slightly.

'That all?' she asked, wondering about the unorthodox training challenge.

'No,' Kate said, pausing to highlight her final point. 'Before you spar, don't give 'em a clue as to what's coming. OK?' Kate licked Nicky's beautiful face, sending exciting shocks through both their bodies.

After thinking about the plan for a moment Nicky finally got the genius-ness of it and with a return lick of Kate's face smiled mischievously.

'You can definitely count on it!'

CHAPTER X

IN less then 24 hours Ravi had the marketing and business aspects of their project all sorted, from the printing of Luv Inc flyers and stickers, to a proactive direct to the public distribution strategy. He'd even uploaded the functioning e-commerce syntax linking the site to his bank account. Not that he expected anyone to actually join the site. This was more of a precaution to disabling any claim Ryan and Jane's project might have to pip his at the post for first-class honours due to a technicality.

He arrived at Will's apartment with bundles of flyers and stickers in hand to share the moment with his new partner. So far, he found his first actual business enterprise in Australia, although just a College experiment, quite stimulating yet culturally challenging. Had his parents back home in Karachi known it was a western dating site offering free condoms as an inducement to join, man, he didn't want to go there even via Fantasy Land.

Like a child, Will began to play with the stickers as soon as Ravi arrived, even cunningly sticking one on Ravi's back as he looked the other way. Strangely, it was acceptable today, as the promotional aspect that Will chose from the marketing book Ravi had loaned him demanded every ounce of childlike playfulness they could muster.

Their first port of call was to attend a costume hire shop. Will had chosen a foam heart-shaped bodysuit complete with red gloves, boots and a hat. He played with himself in front of the mirror as shop assistant Jenny helped Ravi apply his body and facial make-up for the costume that Will had chosen for him.

Will pissed himself laughing when Ravi came out of the fitting room presenting himself as a pure white, head to toe made up Cupid, complete with wings and a golden bow and arrow. Of course, Will's mockery offended Jenny who thought

---

her application of the make-up was impeccable, which it was. If only she knew Will's IQ was lower than his shoe size it wouldn't have been an issue. What really ticked her off to the max were actually Ravi's covert actions. A dozen or so Luv Inc stickers were found plastered all over the dressing rooms and mirrors not long after the costumed Indian Cupid and the Big Love Heart had left the building, armed with Luv Inc flyers and stickers ready to pass out to the Brisbane city masses.

After a few hours of dishing out flyers on street corners, subway tunnels, and in food courts, Ravi had been surprised at how receptive busy city workers were to receiving their material. He put it down to the comedy factor. Most of the approaching public who'd looked up to notice him had smiles on their faces by the time they reached him. *What harm could an Indian Cupid or a smiling Heart do?* he reasoned with himself. Oddly enough, the credit belonged to Will's marketing selections and he made a mental note not to forget to praise his partner when the working day was over.

Ravi's pleasant thoughts peaked just before shopping mall security guards detained him, handing him over to the police within record time. Handcuffed, he was then escorted to a nearby police station where he was shown the evidence of the complaint. He had no defence as security camera footage showed Cupid Ravi entering and then exiting a ladies restroom with less Luv Inc stickers in his hands than he had when he had first entered. How embarrassment!

As the cell door was being closed behind Ravi, Will was still on the city streets and having a ball. It was the first time in his life women had actually returned his smile and responded pleasantly to his greeting with something other than a, 'Get lost, you geek creep!' Shit, he was even thinking of keeping the costume and forfeiting his deposit, when he suddenly felt his groin vibrating. He took off a glove to retrieve his cell

---

phone but had trouble putting it to his ear due to his oversized costume. He thought the call was a prank until he heard it was a police officer. 'We need you to come down to the station to verify his identity and bail him out.'

'Yes officer,' Will replied.

His mind raced with cop shop scenarios but as he made his way to the station it changed to how peeved he was to have his best flirting day ever disrupted by this inconvenience. He decided to detour to get lunch and a beer and to give Ravi time to reflect on his misdemeanour.

The desk cops tried to hold back their laughter with great difficulty when, true to Ravi's word, in walked a Big Love Heart through the precinct doors and up to the counter requesting bail for Cupid. Truth be told, Ravi could have been released on bail under his own undertaking but when he explained his and Will's costumed mission, they unearthed an irresistible opportunity to provide the station with a gag for the day moment, with even the Duty Sergeant in on it.

They decided to catch the train back to their campus and used the opportunity to pass out more stickers and flyers. On board their train, covered in shit, aches, and pains, was Nicky's workmate Neil, who accepted the sticker before putting it into his workbag. While catching her connecting bus home from school, Alex noticed one of the Luv Inc flyers abandoned at her stop and she also put it into her schoolbag.

Back on campus, Will and Ravi's workday was not over. After re-applying make-up to his face and hands, Ravi continued to dish out fresh stickers around Robinson while Will did a car park run, leaving flyers under 1000 or so windscreen wipers.

Once again, Cupid Ravi couldn't resist entering the ladies restrooms to leave his mark and almost bowled over three female students as he exited the one located inside the law faculty. Unfortunately for Luv Inc one of the girls that was nearly bowled over was the girlfriend of a high-ranking Alpha member and news quickly got back to Ryan Davis who considered the duos actions a most insolent rebuke to his café announcement and anti Salt'n'Pepper party. Ryan had all three girls make a formal complaint in writing to Dean Chester.

By the time they got back to Will's apartment the sun was setting and they were both totally exhausted. Will went to his bedroom to change out of his costume while Ravi took a seat on the lounge after taking off his Cupid wings and setting his golden bow and arrow down. By the time Will came back from the kitchen with a beer Ravi was stretched out sound asleep and snoring. He retrieved a blanket from the closet and flung it over Ravi wondering how much of his white body make-up would end up on his lounge in the morning. He only got half way through his beer before he too felt the overwhelming urge to crash.

*****

Late the following day after nothing had been done to remedy their written grievances, Ryan had the girls refuel the charge along with a report from the janitor and a graffiti complaint. A little over the top, perhaps, but it was a better alternative than losing face before his fellow Alpha fraternity members and groupies. Besides, their website challenge had filtered throughout every faculty of Robinson College and nothing short of Will and Ravi being sent to summer school purgatory would quell his retribution. Chester received the complaint too late into the afternoon to speak to anyone about it and so put it onto his "To Resolve" pile as he left work for the day.

Chapter XI

AT the industrial repair shop Neil showed Bob the Luv Inc sticker while they were on lunch. They came up with a master plan in five seconds flat and figured the laugh from tempting the wrath of Nicky once again was worth the risk. While Bob played lookout Neil crept into the car park and planted the sticker onto the bumper of Nicky's 4WD.

After work they managed to get out before her and sprinted to their pre-planned hiding position: and then they waited. When they spotted Nicky exiting the building they ducked down so quickly that they bumped their heads and then nearly missed her getting into her 4WD. Already late for training, Nicky started the car and took off, the squealing wheels passing right by the duo's hiding spot. Bob couldn't resist getting a better look and stood up as she drove away. Had Nicky glanced at her rear-vision mirror she would have noticed the boys bursting at the seams with how much they were laughing, pointing at her rear end and high-fiving each other.

Later that night Nicky and Kate left the Dojo together after an exhausting training session. As they approached Nicky's 4WD Kate was the one who spotted the sticker on the bumper.

'Are you cheating on me?' she said, acting hurt and directing her young gun's attention to the sticker.

'What the fuck!' Nicky exclaimed as she ripped the freshly applied sticker from her bumper. She took a mental shot of the bright red Luv Inc logo before scrunching it up and throwing it into the nearby bushes. Knowing someone had taken the piss, Kate's continuous teasing and smirking started to drive Nicky a little wild. She jumped into the driver's seat and started the car, but didn't open the passenger door just yet. She revved the engine then put her stereo on. LOUD.

After ten seconds Kate tapped on the passenger window

wanting to get into the car. Finally, Nicky turned the music down then responded to the tap on the glass by simply winding down the window.

'Feel like walking?' This was enough to silence Kate and her teasing.

*****

At precisely the same time, Alex was locked away in her bedroom surfing the Luv Inc website. The 10 free babysitting vouchers on the benefits page excited her. The other clinching factor on the road to making her decision was the 50% off cinemas and restaurants offer.

With her diabolical plan completed it was time for its practical execution. Alex silently opened her bedroom door, tiptoed down the hall then halted to take a peek around the corner. She saw her dad asleep and snoring in front of the television. Perfect! She continued down the hallway to his bedroom and found his wallet in a drawer next to his bed. She opened it, took out his credit card then replaced the wallet into the drawer and snuck back out.

With the booty in hand she retraced her steps and paused once again. She looked up at the last piece of the puzzle, a framed photo of her dad. Too high for her to reach she went into her bedroom, picked up her desk chair and returned. Stealthily, she placed the chair on the floor in front of the picture, stood up and retrieved the photo. Placing one foot on the floor she nearly dropped the photo when the TV switched to a loud commercial that also aroused John momentarily. Had he awoke and looked over his shoulder he would have busted her in mid heist. She froze without taking a breath until the program came back on and she could hear him start to snore again. With the chair in one hand and the picture in the other, she returned to her den of deceit and back to work.

The Luv Inc site had her firstly set up a member profile. A

---

quick scan of her dad's photo, a few answers as to what her dad liked and disliked and wanted… well, more like what she wanted and was looking for in a replacement mum, but she was sure he wanted the same thing, and she was nearly done. Then came the only hard part—what to call him? She thought hard and then had an idea when she remembered his favourite film franchise.

Finally, to complete her mission Alex had to enter John's credit card details. This gave her project a sense of urgency as she realised that since he received his bank statements monthly she'd have to get him to go out on first date before he saw Luv Inc in black and white on his next statement.

'Here we go,' she whispered, as she double clicked the Submit icon.

A knock on her door made her jump, then spring to action. She slammed her laptop shut and hid the credit card and photo underneath her sheets.

'Can I come in?' her dad asked.

'Sure,' she replied, before diving onto her bed just as the door swung open.

'What's doing, Sweet Pea?'

'Just a little school project. All done now,' she fibbed.

'Time to tuck in,' he said, and he put a hand on her quilt ready to pull it back for her.

She sprang to her feet and turned the lights off and then jumped into the bed, the darkness hiding the evidence under the sheets.

'I could have done that for you on the way out, sweetie,' he said, as she adjusted her pillows.

'Kiss?' she asked, avoiding his comment.

'See you in the morning. Goodnight,' he said, pecking her on the cheek.

She waited till he had closed the door behind him to answer with a sly smile.

'Goodnight, John_007!'

*****

On the other side of town Nicky had gotten home, stripped to her underwear and was sitting on her lounge typing her details into Luv Inc.'s Ideal Matchmaker software.

Q: What type of men are you looking for?
A: Young kickboxers.
Q: What type of relationship are you looking for?
A: One night stands.
Q: How would you describe yourself?
A: Dangerously sexy!

Then came the last request on the page: Submit at least one photo of yourself here. Nicky reached for her phone then browsed through her album looking for a photo that matched her Dangerously Sexy profile, but she could find none that quite fit. Determined to get her profile just right she resolved the situation by taking a selfie on her phone via her wall mirror. FLASH!

When her eyes came back after being blinded by the flash she studied her self-portrait, which unfortunately also showed the phone in her hand. *What a desperado!* she thought, and in a flash devised another photo option. Without putting a stitch of extra clothing on she exited the apartment in her underwear and knocked on her neighbour's door. It didn't take long for Ted to answer—not after he'd gotten a good look at her through his peephole!

'Hi Ted, I need a photo. Do you mind?' Nicky threw him her cell phone before he could answer,

'Sure,' he said, delightedly licking his lips.

Nicky got into a classic boxing pose that showed off all her muscles, yet didn't hide her breast assets, and smiled. FLASH! All done! Ted just stood there hypnotised by the image on Nicky's phone until she grabbed it back from his vice like grip. Annoyed, she started to leave but then had another thought and turned back round.

'Say Ted, have you ever done any kickboxing?'

'Never. But I'll try anything once,' he replied.

'Really? How much medical insurance do you have?' she chuckled, turning around and giving Ted another serve of her delicious rump-in-thong before returning to her apartment.

Nicky connected her phone to her computer and uploaded the photo straight to her profile. *Finger licking good*, she thought to herself until she clicked on the Submit button.

'FIVE HUNDRED BUCKS! My, my, are you boys going to cop a pounding,' she snarled, and with ferocious anticipation she entered the digits of her credit card.

Like many other Luv Inc punters from the four corners of Brisbane city Nicky went to bed with visions and dreams. However, the major differences separating their fantasies from hers involved them hoping for "Love & Romance" while she was envisioning "Pain & Anguish;" them imagining gifts of "Perfume & Roses" while she was inflicting "Black Eyes & Bruises;" and them dreaming of "Wedding Cake & Kids' while she was in the ring "Fucking-Up Her Nemesis!"

CHAPTER XII

AFTER a candle lit dinner Ravi went to bed early, but not to his bed. He had conversation and some catch-up love to make up to his secret girlfriend. Why secret? Well this was another portion of his life in Australia that, had his family back home in Pakistan known anything about, would have had him disowned in a flash. His girlfriend also had a bit at stake by their affair but for her it was well worth their risky business. Ravi was quite the accommodating gentleman both in manner and between the sheets, but who would have thought that just by looking at him? For this, she was grateful as it ensured Ravi was all hers.

The next morning on the way back from her place Ravi stopped off to withdraw cash from an ATM. As the rising sun reflected light off the screen he tapped in his PIN and waited for his cash to be dispensed. He first took his cash and then his transaction receipt, checking the balance before going to throw it in the bin. He rubbed his eyes then took another look at the balance on the receipt this time bringing it closer, a lot closer.

'It can't be,' he whispered to himself; but he had to make sure. He marched into the branch proper and took a position in the queue.

'How can I help you today, Sir?' Mary, his teller, greeted him with her most pleasant smile.

'I would like to check my account balance please.'

'Certainly. Do you have your card?' she asked.

Ravi fumbled a little before passing the card to her, then looked around suspiciously. Mary continued to smile as she swiped his card but all the while kept a nervous eye on him. When his balance came up on the screen she too became a little edgy.

49

'Do you have any ID on you, Sir?' she asked.

Ravi fumbled through his wallet once again and handed over his driver's licence. After checking the photo she was sure she had done all that was required to ensure security, according to banking policy. She passed the licence back to Ravi.

'Would you like me to print out a statement for you, Mr. Ali?'

Ravi nodded. Ten seconds later she passed both the receipt and his ATM card back to him.

'Is there anything else I can do for you today, Sir?'

Ravi couldn't remember the last time someone called him sir. He answered Mary with a shake of the head then turned to exit.

He waited until he was around the corner to check the printout he had just received. At that moment his world started to crumble and his stomach began to ache. He'd never been in trouble with the law before but on numerous occasions he'd seen how lawbreakers in Pakistan were treated and he was scared. The shame of deportation and look of disappointment on his parents' faces crossed his mind while the mirage of having to spend the rest of his life working for his family in an overcrowded Karachi left him limp. He didn't go directly home but walked around for a while thinking about what to do before an idea with a name and face popped into his head: Will Jackson!

*****

Trish Bain and James Rosenthal were seated and waiting in Dean Chester's reception with questions of their own. Miss Green finally called them into the Dean's office where the sombre faced Chester greeted and ushered them to the chairs in front of his desk. He handed them both copies of the complaints from the female students as well as the one from the janitor.

'We received these official complaints yesterday and had they not been in writing I'd have been happy to let them just blow over. I've made some inquiries this morning and they have come back to me indicating that the students involved are in your classes. Is that correct?'

Rosenthal speed-read all the documents before replying.

'I have no idea, but for the record, I do view this as very advantageous marketing.'

'Yes, it could be seen that way,' Chester replied, 'It's just a shame a few students feel it's more like an invasion of their privacy.'

Trish read the words "Cupid Indian" in her copy of the reports and then looked up at both men.

'Ravi Ali.'

'How can you be so sure, Trish?'

'While I can't confirm the bathroom incident, I can affirm Luv Inc as his and Will Jackson's combined project,' she answered.

'I see,' Chester paused. 'Do we have any ideas as to how to make this all go away before parents and benefactors get involved?'

Due to the triviality of the complaints both lecturers looked at each other slightly baffled.

'What are your thoughts?' Rosenthal asked, attempting to distance himself from the final solution.

Chester's hands were somewhat tied. This was mainly due to Robinson being a private for profit enterprise, with so many more classified eyes prying into his responsibilities than when he was once a college student. Some of these were also the relatives of his students. If this ever went any further he needed proof that he'd conducted the investigation by the book. Chester pushed a button on the intercom on his desk.

'Miss Green, can you come in with a notepad please?'

'Yes, Sir,' she replied, and was in there in a flash.

*****

Will wasn't used to getting woken up by his front door being all-but busted down.

'OK, OK, I'M COMING!' he yelled, annoyed. As he walked through his lounge he noticed Abigail was also restless due to the thumping vibrations. When he opened the door Ravi bowled him over like a riot cop with a search warrant as he rushed into the room. 'Good morning to you too!'

Ravi began to pace Will's lounge room.

'YOU SEE?' Ravi accused, holding the statement up as evidence.

'See what?' Will retorted, bemused.

'I am truly in the deep shit now without a shovel!' Ravi cried.

'Calm down, Slugger. What you got there?' Will asked as he closed the door.

'This is the bank statement for Luv Inc for the last 48 hours.'

Will snatched it from him as he wiped the sleep out of his eyes. He read it once, twice and then screamed.

'ONE HUNDRED AND FORTY-THREE THOUSAND DOLLARS!!! NO WAY!'

Will kissed the statement like it was Wonka's Golden Ticket.

'Yes way, and it gets worse, much worse,' Ravi continued.

'Worse, how?' Will questioned.

'William, I'm only in this country on a student visa. If immigration find out I have been trading as a businessman I will be deported!'

'At least you'll be flying back first class,' Will said sarcastically.

'And if my referral calculations are correct,' Ravi continued, 'we'll have close to one thousand members and five hundred thousand in cash by the end of next month.'

Will looked at Ravi like he was insane.

'Am I seriously misunderstanding something?'

Ravi couldn't believe his lack of empathy, so he had to get his attention some other way.

'William, you're sailing on this sinking ship too, my friend.'

'You've got to be joking! How?' Will asked, now more attentive.

Ravi looked him in the eye.

'Do we own a company or are we registered for sales taxes?

'No,' Will replied.

'That's tax evasion, maximum five years in prison. Do we have agreements with any restaurants, cinemas or babysitting services?'

'I tried to tell you —'

'FALSE advertising, another indictable offence,' Ravi continued, ignoring Will. 'Do we have any condoms?'

'I don't use them myself but what's your point?' Will chuckled, still not quite comprehending the seriousness of the situation, nor his part at its centre.

'My point is that unless we fix the aforementioned issues at an expeditious speed we are going directly to jail and I'll be returning to Pakistan with a criminal record!'

Will stood there with a poker face. Finally the light bulb above his head went off. He held up an index finger.

'Hold that thought.'

Will jumped feet first onto his lounge then began bouncing on it like a trampoline.

'FIVE…HUNDRED…THOUSAND…HOLY…CATFISH… DOLLARS…BATMAN!!!'

Ravi looked down and made eye contact with Will's tarantula. He wondered, if she could talk, what other bizarre chronicles could she reveal about her off-the-wall captor? He spun around just as Will returned to earth, out of breath and still clutching the bank statement.

'Can we at least spend the money first?' he asked, as if prepared to do the time after profiting from the crime.

Ravi shook his head at his ridiculous comeback.

'William, I have no plans to go to jail, nor to spend the money. I have been walking around for hours and have come up with a plan that, with a little intelligent help from you, might get us out of this predicament.'

A loud knock at the door stopped Will from answering.

'Who is it?' Will shouted.

'Trish Bain,' came the muffled reply.

'Trish who?'

'Miss Bain. My lecturer,' Ravi answered.

'What's she doing here?' Will asked.

'Just open the door,' Ravi moaned.

'Come in,' Will said as he opened the door.

'Thanks. Hi, Ravi. Hey, nice tarantula,' she commented as she passed Abigail's tank.

'So what can I do for you?' Will asked, slightly unhinged that she was inside his apartment.

'Actually, it's what I have done for you two!' she replied, then handed Will an official Robinson University letter.

'The dean has suspended us!' he exclaimed after reading the front page.

Ravi snatched the letter from Will's grip.

'What?' he said, and began to read it.

'You haven't been suspended, yet, but he's given you til 5pm to get rid of every Luv Inc sticker on College grounds or you will be,' Trish clarified.

'It says here he has confiscated all of the access codes for the site.' Ravi looked up from the indictment.

'He wanted the power to shut you down if you didn't comply with the order,' Trish said.

'I can't believe after bailing you out the other day you're BANG, right back into women's toilets!' Will accused, finally having some ammunition on his partner.

'You had to be bailed out?' Trish asked.

Ravi turned as red-faced as a coloured man could. He took Trish by the arm and led her to the door.

'Can we have this conversation some other time please? As you have now briefed us we have much work to do. Thank you for stopping by,' he finished, politely.

Trish was offended but held her peace.

'Fine. But if I were you I'd find those girls in that report and appease their complaints before word gets out, you understand? Oh, and perhaps the janitor as well,' she concluded before she exited.

Ravi closed the door behind her and put his hand into his pocket, pulling out a bundle of $100 notes.

'Here take this,' he said, snatching the bank statement out of Will's hand and replacing it with the bundle of green cash.

'What's this for?' Will queried before starting to count the wad of bills.

'Find and make peace with the girls in the complaint. I'll take care of the janitor and the stickers.' Ravi opened the door to leave then turned back to his business partner. 'I have some ideas to get us out of this sticky jam; give me a day or two to work on them, OK?' he asked. Ravi put a hand out to Will, which he accepted and shook.

'OK, partner,' Will replied, and closed the door. He already had an idea about how to appease the girls in the complaint and if it went to plan, boy, were they going to get a surprise and a half!

*****

Unbeknownst to Ravi and Will, they weren't the only ones in on the out-of-the blue success of Luv Inc. Their site's hard drive had been invaded overnight by Françoise Acolyte, AKA Hacker, a computer geek who worked for another singles dating site: Up2U.com.

This job wasn't 22-year-old Hacker's ideal vocation, however, it was a great start in his newly adopted country. He did this dirty deed mainly to get the attention of his boss, Randall Stevens, who didn't seem to pay his employees according to the standard of his own lavish lifestyle.

Hacker thought his covert operation might be a great attitude adjuster before asking for a pay rise. He was at his workstation with the LuvInc.com data open on his screen when Randall arrived.

'What's so urgent?' he asked Hacker, as if his time was of royal preciousness.

'Take ze look at ziss,' Hacker replied with his thick Parisian accent.

Randall looked at the Luv Inc page on Hacker's screen. 'LuvInc.com. What a stupid name!'

'Zey have tree hundra member join in ze last 48 hour,' Hacker added to make his case.

'So?' Randall said, not taking in this trivial statistic.

'It's ze quality not quantity, no?' Hacker tapped the keyboard and brought up the member page. As Randall read it, Hacker noticed his facial expressions change and knew he'd gotten the point across.

'FIVE HUNDRED DOLLARS!' he exclaimed.

Now was Hacker's time to prove his worth.

'I hack into zair data base and zey have already sign up 95 of our oldest clients.'

Hacker could almost hear the number crunching cogs turning in Randall's mind and he made a bet with himself on exactly what the next words would be that passed Randall's lips.

'So who else knows about this?' Randall demanded.

Hacker could feel the extra cash from his pay rise in his pocket already.

'Just you and me, Patron.' he guaranteed, using the French word for boss to assure him of his discretion.

'Good, keep it that way. Print out everything you can on this crew and get it to me personally. ASAP. Understood?'

'Why, of course,' Hacker replied, obligingly.

Randall patted him on the back before returning to his office with a furrowed brow and a plan already forming in his mind.

*****

Ravi entered the janitor's office at Robinson to extend his hand to the head of maintenance, Ralph Hansard. Embarrassed, he confessed his deeds and stopped Ralph's condescending tone in mid speech by slapping hundred dollar bills into his open palm. Ralph was glad he'd sent the rest of his staff to lunch. He assured Ravi that not only would they have every Luv Inc sticker gone by 5pm, but also that the incident would disappear from his staff's memories as well.

Oddly, it was the first occasion in Australia that Ravi felt empowered by having a pocket full of cash. He started to understand a little about the supremacy Ryan Davis must feel as Alpha's top gun. His thoughts then turned to how grand it was going to be when Luv Inc took top class honours and at the same time knocked Ryan off his high horse.

There's nothing sweeter than sweet revenge, he kept repeating in his mind as he shook hands with Ralph.

*****

Will had to wait until after dark to activate his appeasement project. Following an afternoon reconnaissance mission to find out where the girls lived, he waited around the corner of their share house until his surprise turned up.

About ten minutes later a 4WD pulled over to the curb with a screech. The window rolled down revealing a well-built and perfectly tanned male driver.

'You're Will, yeah?' he asked.

Will answered in the affirmative then handed Ben five hundred dollars and a Luv Inc sticker. He explained his instructions expecting them to be obeyed to the letter. Ben assured him that they were nothing out of the ordinary for his profession and for a cash job he'd be glad to throw in a bonus or two.

Alyssa, Jane, and Bianca were putting their dinner plates into the dishwasher when the doorbell rang.

'You expecting anyone?' Alyssa asked the other two girls.

They both answered with a shake of the head. Alyssa went to the front door, opened it, and gasped. Standing there dressed as Zorro and holding a portable CD player was none other than Ben the Strip-O-Gram.

'Are you Bianca, Jane or Alyssa?' he asked.

'Alyssa,' she replied, then bit her lip.

'I have the right address then. You girls ready for a show?' he asked, before pushing play on the CD player and entering the apartment.

Alyssa's wolf whistles and cheers drew Jane and Bianca from the kitchen faster than ever. As they dashed in to see what the fuss was all about they saw Alyssa sitting front and centre on the lounge wearing Zorro's cape, as a half naked Ben danced on the coffee table. Mesmerised, they took a seat on either side of her as Ben finished unbuttoning his shirt.

Two songs later, Jane was holding Zorro's sword while Bianca was on her knees with a long-stemmed red rose in her mouth trying to unlace the stud's boots.

In the finale, Ben kept his word to Will. As he stood on the coffee table with only his pants on, he put a thumb into the top of his pants and gestured with his other hand to see if they wanted the Full Monty. All three screamed and clapped their approval in unison. To highlight his next move Ben turned around then ripped his custom dance pants off in a flash revealing the Luv Inc sticker plastered over the cheeks of his G-stringed buns before horse-slapping himself numerous times as a confession to being a very naughty boy.

Alyssa bravely got up to detach the sticker but Ben noticed her move and before she could do anything with that hand, he snatched it and hid it under the hat he had by now placed over his bulging groin.

When Ben left the next morning, he didn't know who had removed the sticker but he assured Will by phone that after such a response from his audience, it would never have ended up in the rubbish bin.

CHAPTER XIII

CHESTER waited until Laura was in the bathroom to enter his study. He sat at his computer and typed in www.luvinc.com and pressed return. It was the first time in his life he'd ever laid eyes on such a web presence. He was astounded how inviting the members' pictures were and how easy it was to navigate to the Over 50's section. He clicked onto the profile picture of an attractive blonde. Up came a window instructing him that if he wished to see her other profile pictures he'd have to create a profile with a picture of his own.

Chester got up and started to pace his study floor. He passed the screen a few times then looked up to a picture of himself hanging on the wall that was taken in the 90s. The feeling he was experiencing time warped him to his teenage school camps where, from under their sleeping bags, his tent buddies would torch-light photos and magazines they had "borrowed" from their dads and big brothers to share with the others. After he'd taken his picture down he tried to convince himself that it was just to look at the profiles and that he could never jump the fence into actually contacting anyone. However, with the access codes in his pocket from Trish Bain—who had confiscated them from Will and Ravi's project file—it was a "free ride" he could justify if busted: all in the name of Academia and Social Science.

*****

Alex had already picked up the skills to email other users as well as how to use the pop-up instant conversation mode to contact them. She then came across JoJo_27 whose profile picture looked like a wax museum copy of her late mother.

Joan, AKA JoJo_27, was in her bedroom dressed for bed when she heard the—TING—informing her that she had Luv Inc mail. She opened it and immediately gave John's profile picture the thumbs-up. His, or rather, Alex's message was flashing on the screen waiting for a response:

Sender: John007
Receiver: JoJo_27
Message: Hi JoJo, this is John. I just wanted to tell you how much I liked your profile and picture. If you like mine, perhaps we could have a chat?

Joan put her hairbrush down and took a seat in front of her computer. She started to go through his profile liking nearly everything she saw, except for the fact that he was nearly 10 years older than she and still single. She needed reassurance he wasn't a player. Her long brown hair tickled the small of her back as she began to type in her response.

*****

Nicky was sitting cross-legged on her bed and whistling as she surfed the Luv Inc site looking for a target. She was so sure she'd get one on the first night that she'd already moved most of her lounge room furniture into her spare room in preparation for her their first date.

She came across the profile of 20-year-old Thomas Braun, 5'10, 72 kg, a third year carpentry apprentice, but most importantly a kickboxing hobbyist. Perfect! Nicky noticed that he was also online. She opened the instant conversation mode box and began to type.

Sender: Tricky_Nicky69
Receiver: TomFun01
Message: Hey babe wanna chat???

Nicky pressed send and counted backwards from 30. When she reached 11 his response came up and was flashing on her screen. *Hello, peeping Tom, you've been a very, very naughty boy,* Nicky smiled as she started to type to her first victim.

*****

Chester was again pacing his study but this time he had his rosary beads out rubbing them feverishly. He stopped before his computer looking down to study his homework.

User Name:	Ready_&_Able51
Occupation:	Travelling Salesman
Interests/Hobbies:	Fishing
Looking For:	Casual Encounters

His profile also included the photo taken 20 years ago. As he sat there staring at the Upload icon he felt her presence and spun round. His heart pounded as Laura, now parked in the study's doorway, returned his stare.

'You frightened me,' he said catching his breath.

'Help me into bed,' she said in her usual monotone.

Chester was relieved she could only see the screen side on.

'I'll be there in a minute,' he said, to buy some time so he could minimise Luv Inc from the screen.

As Laura wheeled off down the hall Chester let out his breath, his heart still pumping blood through his veins at 180 BPM. He stared at the Upload icon for the longest minute of his life. Finally, he clicked the mouse and his journey into the world of internet dating hurtled past the point of no return.

*****

Alex had fun making small talk with Joan yet she was a little surprised how quickly she was prepared to give out her personal info like occupation, what suburb she lived in, and what she'd like to do on a first date. Joan thought some of the questions a little presumptuous but she liked John's bold confidence and since they were both mature and looking for the same result, *Why beat around the bush?* Besides, she had been single for nearly two years and hadn't even been kissed goodnight since, but now it was her turn to ask questions.

Sender: JoJo_27
Receiver: John007
Message: So do you date much?

Sender: John007
Receiver: JoJo_27
Message: Never

A cute guy like you never dates. Yeah right, she thought, *what BS*. She delved deeper — she wanted the truth.

Sender: JoJo_27
Receiver: John007
Message: Why Not???

Alex was prepared for this question. She knew from Sally's advances and Miss Pearle's giggles during parent teacher interviews that John was Hot Property. Firstly she had to put herself into the equation; she'd learnt this from a guidebook borrowed from the library entitled "Mature Dating." "No Surprises" was the chapter she'd taken her notes from.

Sender: John007
Receiver: JoJo_27
Message: Busy working and looking after my 13- year-old daughter.

Someone on the rebound was the last thing Joan needed in her emotional life. She was prepared to finish it then and there but thought it best to let him seal his own fate.

Sender: JoJo_27
Receiver: John007
Message: Divorced or separated???

She waited for his answer but nothing could have prepared her for how guilty she felt when she read it.

Sender: John007
Receiver: JoJo_27
Message: Neither. My wife died a year ago from cancer.

*****

Nicky had already passed through the small talk with Thomas and was going in for the kill. *Men are so predictable*, she thought, *the slightest smell of potential sex and they're all in.*

Sender: Tricky_Nicky69
Receiver: TomFun01
Message: Up for a romantic dinner tomorrow night? My buy — dessert at my place!

Tom assumed he'd hit the jackpot. He thought he'd play the shy boy to test if she was for real.

Sender: TomFun01
Receiver: Tricky_Nicky69
Message: What's the rush? I'm not that easy :-)

'Oh yes you are!' Nicky said to herself. She typed in her answer, powered down her laptop and jumped into bed not the slightest bit concerned that Tom would resist.

Sender: Tricky_Nicky69
Receiver: TomFun01
Message: 355 Main Ave, 7 sharp xxoo

Tom punched the air when he read her message. He sent back his confirmation and left his bedroom to share the good news with his recently arrived Italian flat mate, Carlo.

*****

Although Laura was now tucked up in bed Chester locked the door to his study before turning his attention back to the computer. What he read made his heart skip a beat: "YOU HAVE FIVE NEW MESSAGES" was flashing on his screen. Each message had a thumbnail photo of the sender and he chose one from a brunette whose user name was ThanksGiver54, leading him to think she was perhaps from the United States. He clicked on the Read Letter icon. *A poem, how nice,* he thought.

Sender: ThanksGiver54
Receiver: Ready_and_Able51
Message: You're free to come over,
Either late or early;
As long as you promise,
To stuff my turkey!

Chester was glad he didn't have any drink in his mouth, as he was positive he'd have sprayed his computer screen with it once he'd understood exactly what kind of turkey she was talking about! He navigated back to his profile page and clicked onto the mail from Pretty_N_Pink.

Sender: Pretty_N_Pink
Receiver: Ready_and_Able51
Message: Hi Honey, I read your profile and noticed you are a travelling salesman. Good, I'm looking for something casual and just wanted you to know that next time you're in town you have a bed and breakfast waiting for you!

Chester's naivety hadn't prepared him for how forward and to the point single women who were over 50 would be. *What an untapped market,* he thought, and then remembered that Luv Inc was his students' site and that this was all just a University experiment.

He got up and starting pacing the floor once more. He recounted that it had been 10 years since he and Laura had last made love: how could he forget? He wished the schoolgirl he'd met forty years ago would come back to life. He fantasised about those drives they used to take when they were young and in love but that would never happen again.

He stopped pacing and turned his attention to his screen. Enough was enough! He was a man after all and it was time to step up to the plate and show these woman the fabric he was made of before the only gusto left to share was arthritis, medication and memories.

*****

Joan had to pull herself away from reading John's profile once more. She had that feeling of intense infatuation and didn't want to fall off the reality map so soon.

It was like he'd read her mind when he'd suggested meeting for dinner the Saturday after next. She couldn't wait to share the news with her best friend Suzy, who was actually starting to worry about her lack of trust in men since her last fractured breakup. She powered down her computer after wishing John_007 sweet dreams and jumped into bed with his profile picture plastered firmly in her mind.

She switched on her clock radio and reached into her bedside draw for "Mr Snuggleupagus." She turned out the light and hit the 'ON' and 'Low Speed' buttons, bringing Snuggie up past her knees and over the inside of her thighs: at first only feeling a tingle, and then feeling so much more.

Her "Mmmmm...John Baby" voice was definitely at higher pitch than the monotone hum of her faithful bed friend.

CHAPTER XIV

RAVI had hardly slept in the last two days. His girlfriend assured him that before he could pitch Will a business offer he couldn't refuse leases, agreements, staff and contracts all had to be in place and rubber stamped. He also had the stress of keeping his web creation crash free and up to date. On top of this the thought that his student visa was in jeopardy also played on his nerves.

His biggest learning curve was acquiring the discipline to stay humble and meek as his massive bank account continued to grow and multiply by the hour. His girlfriend had given him every relevant, first-hand business and professional contact she could muster, and a personal guarantee to them that he had the cash to move every deal forward immediately. However, it still did surprise him when the principal of each firm attended their meetings, from the real estate company for Luv Inc.'s new offices to the chairman of one of the top law firms in Brisbane. The saying "Money Talks but Cash Screams" had come true before his very eyes.

Ravi picked Will up from outside his apartment and explained a little about the new home for Luv Inc during the short trip to the office. He held back the most vital staff details wanting Will to meet everybody first before starting the real pitching.

'Why do we need an office?' Will asked, quickly followed by, 'Why wasn't I invited to the interviews? Aren't we supposed to be partners?'

Ravi was glad he'd chosen an office in the closest industrial estate to Robinson College he could find, as five more minutes of Will's questions would have sent him over the edge. Ravi parked close to the front entrance of the single story building, got out and spread his arms wide.

'So what do you think partner?' he asked Will.

'Not bad. Could have been closer to the take-away shop though,' Will responded.

'Come inside and meet the staff,' Ravi said, gesturing for Will to take the lead.

They approached a sign-writer who was busy working on the front door. Will inspected the www.LuvInc.com sign he was about to apply and nodded his approval. They passed by the vacant reception area and entered the main office floor where Will stopped in his tracks. He was taken aback, firstly by the vast size of their floor space and secondly by the buzz of the dozen or so workers from furniture removalists to telephone technicians who were putting the last pieces of the whole shebang together.

Ravi led him to the first occupied cubicle where a business shirt and tied gentleman was unpacking a box of books. When he saw Ravi, he stopped and looked up with a smile. Ravi introduced him.

'This is Martin Truman, head of Luv Inc.'s Sales and Marketing division.'

'So nice to meet you Mr. Jackson. I'm looking forward to working with you,' Martin responded then took Will's hand and shook it.

'Likewise,' Will said. As the duo strolled to continue their inspection Will commented with excitement in his voice, 'He knows my name!'

'Of course he knows your name, you are his boss,' Ravi said wanting to make his partner fully understand his status within the office.

The next occupied cubicle was decorated like a film set from Star Trek. Its occupant, Seth Lipton, was a twenty-something, gum-chewing, techno-head, casually dressed in a tracksuit, baseball cap and joggers. As his bosses inspected the four aligned PCs he was busy connecting to each other Seth didn't even notice their presence courtesy of the headphones he was wearing and the beats they were pounding into his ears.

'Don't let his busy-ness put you off. Seth is one of the best computer technicians in the country and comes highly recommended,' said Ravi.

The next cubicle was a cosy setup that included indoor plants, a small library, a two-seater leather lounge and a coffee table. Its occupant was a smartly dressed Celene Bayer, who perked up and stood to attention with a radiant smile when she noticed them. Will beat her to the punch.

'Well, hello there,' he panted, appreciatively.

'William, let me introduce you to Miss Celene Bayer, our merchandising and accounts coordinator.'

'Pleasure to meet you, Mr. Jackson,' she said, offering Will her hand.

'The pleasure's all mine,' Will said as he shook it.

'Celene, here, was the creator of the highest grossing point-of-sale campaign in the history of Seven-Eleven and has only recently moved to Brisbane from Melbourne. We were most fortunate she was available to join our team,' Ravi added, hoping the calibre of her credentials would draw out some kind of executive professionalism in Will. Celene reached over her desk and retrieved two small boxes.

'Ravi, I already have two condom companies competing for our business. Which one do you think fits the bill?' she said, holding up the boxes she'd just picked up.

Ravi palmed the decision over to Will for a response. His eyes scanned from the condom boxes in her hands up to Celene's eyes extremely slowly.

'I think we should try them out tonight and give them an answer in the morning!' Will said, grinning wildly.

Celene gave Ravi a "WHAT THE?" look. Embarrassed to the max and without a word, Ravi led Will by the arm away from Celene's cubicle and then steered him in the direction of a nearby hallway. Ravi opened a door that sported a "PRESIDENT" sign and escorted Will inside. Will stood there surveying the office, gob-smacked at the tastefulness of the walnut desk and library shelves supported by a mini-bar, fridge and cappuccino machine, and two leather lounges divided by a wood-grained coffee table.

'Wow, man, you could run the whole country from in here, Slugger!'

Ravi shook his head and pointed to the desk.

'Don't you see? Look closer,' he said.

Will's eyes bulged as he read the gold letters inside the plaque: William Jackson: President.

'You mean it's. . .' Will started.

'Your office my friend!' finished Ravi.

Will stared at the space between the mini-bar and the lounges and pointed.

'I think this is a perfect spot for Abigail.'

Ravi had never heard him mention that name before.

'Who is Abigail?' he asked.

'My tarantula,' Will answered.

Ravi thought for a few seconds.

'How can you tell if it's female?'

'Actually I don't know, I'm just guessing,' Will replied.

Ravi shook his head wondering how they'd gotten onto the topic and off their enterprise.

'Come, we have business to attend to.'

Ravi guided Will down the hallway into an open boardroom where two grey-haired gentlemen in designer suits were awaiting their arrival. The shorter of the two stepped forward with a smile and shook Will's hand.

'Hi there William, Fred Gower attorney at law,' he stated, then passed his business card into Will's proffered hand.

The next gentleman stepped forward.

'Michael Sachs Bean Counter, pleased to make your acquaintance, William.' He offered William his business card to add to his collection.

Ravi offered Will a seat at the head of the table then closed the door. On the table in front of Will's chair were five sets of paperwork bundles all with "Sign Here" Post its on them. Fred Gower opened the proceedings.

'Now, William, you and Ravi are up-and-coming entrepreneurs. I mean I haven't seen such amazing "freak" business prowess like this since the 80s, and our job is to keep you sailing that way for. . . .'

ONE HOUR AND 13 MINUTES LATER...

All of them except Will had taken their ties off, rolled up their sleeves and had large beads of sweat running down their foreheads. Will had insisted on reading each contract from scratch over and over. Michael Sachs had actually given up and was pacing the far end of the boardroom.

'Let me get this straight: I sign this one and I become president of Luv Inc?' Will asked.

'Correct,' Fred Gower affirmed with relief.

'OK... But why is Ravi's name not on it?'

Fred let out a sigh.

'As we've explained, Mr. Ali is in our country on a student visa which means he cannot own or have shares in a private company.'

'I see. And this one?' Will asked again.

This time Michael Sachs answered.

'That is the authority to open a Luv Inc account with you as the sole signatory.'

'And this one?' Will asked, after picking it up from the bundle before him. This time Ravi offered the answer.

'That is a private agreement between you and me. Its power divides and distributes the profits from Luv Inc, 51 precent to you and 49.9 percent to me, making us equal partners.'

Will looked up at Ravi.

'Hang on—doesn't that make us unequal?' he said, not computing that he had the controlling stake.

Ravi picked up a pen angrily, crossed out the percentage figures, changed them to 50/50, signed the contract and passed them to Will to sign. Will lifted his pen off the table finally.

'That's better, now I'm ready to do business,' he said, and began to sign all five contracts. Ravi, Sachs and Cowan all let out sighs of relief.

With all the paperwork tucked safely away in their briefcases, Cowan and Sachs shook hands with Will and were ushered out of the boardroom by Ravi. When they reached the car park, Cowan turned to Ravi and took his hand.

'Congratulations Mr. Ali, I think?' Cowan said with an air of sarcasm.

Sachs also gripped Ravi's hand.

'Good-luck Ravi. I think you're going to need it.'

Ravi concurred as they got into Cowan's car.

'I am totally aware of how much I'm going to need it, gentlemen. Now thank you once again and good day!'

CHAPTER XV

TOM was glad he'd left home 10 minutes early for his date with Nicky. He'd found the address she'd emailed him easy enough but was confused when he recalled that her invitation was for a romantic date. Since 355 Main Avenue turned out to be a Subway Restaurant he continued further along the street looking for something else that fitted the bill. When the next two blocks only contained closed retail shops Tom made an about face and got back to Subway one minute before a seductively dressed Nicky arrived.

'Tom?' she questioned.

'Nicky?' he replied hesitantly, as she leaned toward him to peck him on the cheek.

'I thought you said we were going on a romantic date?' he probed.

'What's not romantic about sharing a Footlong?' she replied with a twinkle in her eye. Tom gulped as Nicky took him by the hand and led him inside.

After he'd selected the ingredients of their Footlong they took a seat in a booth far away from any other customers. Tom had hardly eaten all day and started into his dinner with a bigger than normal bite. Nicky sat quietly observing him but didn't touch the other half of the Footlong that sat on the table. He swallowed.

'You're not hungry?'

Nicky looked up with a cheeky smile.

'Oh I'm hungry alright, just not for food!'

Tom's ears pricked up then unexpectedly, Nicky leaned over the table and whispered in his ear, telling him exactly what she was hungry for. Tom's eyes bulged to bursting and his hands went numb causing him to Ka-Plonk his six-inch onto the table.

Without another word Nicky got up, took him by the hand, and escorted him out of the restaurant and into a cab…

SEVEN MINUTES AND TWENTY-THREE SECONDS LATER…

Nicky opened the door to her apartment and escorted Tom inside then closed the door behind him. He waited in total darkness until she flicked the light-switch on then began to undress in the kitchen. Tom, in total disbelief of his fortune, unlaced and ripped off his shoes then unbuttoned his shirt. By the time he'd taken it off Nicky had already stripped to her G-string and bra and began stretching her legs by bending over and touching the floor in front of her.

Tom's blood started to thump through his veins and after unzipping his jeans he looked around the room for a spot to hang them. This was when he noticed something very strange about the lounge room. There was neither a lounge, a TV, nor a stereo in the room: it was bare except for a large, white martial arts mat in the centre of the floor and an unusual clock on the wall. Not wanting to halt the momentum he threw his jeans onto the kitchen bench and moved in closer to touch her. Nicky bitch-slapped his hand away.

'Not yet. First you have to qualify,' she stated in a new dominatrix tone.

'Qualify for what?'

'My bedroom, of course,' Nicky said, and then with a jolt she pushed him backwards into the middle of the mat.

'Are you serious?' Tom asked in disbelief.

Before he got his response Nicky moved forward and hit a button. The wall timer began to count down from 3.00…2.59…2.58… Nicky spun around to face Tom.

'Three minutes. Kickboxing style. Winner gets to cum first,' she said and shaped up to him like a pro boxer.

Tom's chuckle was erased from his mouth when she attacked,

'KEE-JAH!' Nicky kicked him squarely on the forehead just above his left eye.

'SHIT YOU ARE!' he shrieked, then shaped up to face her.

Nicky faked a low kick to his leg then landed a "SLAP" on his right cheek.

'Bitch!' Tom retorted, as she circled him like a lioness.

'Sorry,' she chuckled, 'but flattery's not getting you out of this one, buddy.' She advanced again, this time with a combination of punches that Tom managed to deflect.

After fending off another advance, Tom tried a combination of his own but Nicky was too fast and deflected each thrust. Then the sweat from his forehead started to run into the open and bloody wound over his left eye. He put a finger to it, all the while keeping an eagle eye on his encircling opponent. Nicky smiled knowing full well the mix of sensations he was feeling. An open flesh wound when mixed with fresh warm sweat and a bruised ego = INTENSE PAIN!

CHAPTER XVI

MAGGIE, AKA ThanksGiver54, was having a quiet night at home on the couch, channel surfing and munching on microwave popcorn and chocolate biscuits. Her apartment was small and cozy forcing her to utilise her lounge room as a combined entertainment and office area. In between handfuls of popcorn a—TING—from her computer made her ears prick. She rose from the lounge with a spring in her step and flashed into her desk chair. She hit a button on the keyboard and the awaiting Luv Inc message opened fully on her screen.

Sender: Ready_and_Able51
Receiver: ThanksGiver54
Message: I don't mean to frighten,
Or wake you from your sleep,
Could I please come over,
Early Monday week?

How cute, Maggie thought, that Ready_and_Able51 had replied to her poem with a poem. She giggled like a schoolgirl who'd just found out her crush was reciprocated. She thought of her reply, licked her lips then began to type.

Chester was feeling the pinch to retire for the night. It had been a long evening of emails to his Luv Inc companions after another long day at the office but before he powered off his computer, the—TING—of ThanksGiver54's return message shattered his silence. He clicked on the message and read.

Sender: ThanksGiver54
Receiver: Ready_and_Able51
Message: I don't know your name,
Or where you go fishin',
Come over and pull me apart,
Like a hot Bar-B-Que chicken!

My God! Chester thought to himself, *What kind of a woman thinks like that?* While still contemplating the answer — TING — another response arrived, this time from Pretty_N_Pink to confirm his request for a rendezvous with her as well. Startled by their rapid responses Chester got up and started to pace the study with a nauseous feeling in his stomach like he was about to be brought in to see his school principal. He took out his rosary beads and began to pray, asking for the mercy to soothe his guilt.

*****

Tom was awakened by a stinging sensation above his left eye. He sprang out of bed and ran into the bathroom. Standing in front of the mirror confirmed his suspicion — a swollen black eye of which only a mutt from a crossbred litter would be proud.

Embarrassed about having to explain to his flatmate how he'd been laid-out by his date he quickly brushed his teeth, dressed for work, put on a pair of his darkest sunglasses and made a dash for the front door. However, halfway to freedom he was confronted by Carlo in the kitchen who was making his usual morning coffee.

'Ciao, Tom You have the hangover, ha-ha?' he questioned with a little laugh.

'Yeah,' Tom replied, shielding the left side of his face to prevent Carlo from getting a side view.

'Tell me all about your hot date,' Carlo continued, genuinely interested in his flatmates intercourse.

'I have to get to work,' Tom said and tried to brush past.

Carlo saw the black patch above his eye and cheek and grabbed him by the arm.

'Amigo, what happened to your face?'

'Nothing,' Tom lied.

'Who hits you?' Carlo asked with a hint of rage in his eyes.

'I'm OK,' Tom assured him.

'What you mean OK? I am your friend, no? Tells me who hits you?' he urged.

Tom had nowhere to run. He dropped his head and confessed.

'It was my date...'

Surprisingly, Carlo let out a belly laugh.

'Ha, Ha! She is the wild woman in the bed, no?' he chuckled while patting Tom on the back. Tom's honesty couldn't hold this type of concealment.

'We had a fight,' he confessed.

Carlo was taken aback.

'You have the fight on the first date?' Carlo questioned. Looking thoughtful for a moment he laughed again as he said, 'Carlo's mama and papa have the fight on the first date! Is good luck no?'

He slapped Tom on the back once more for encouragement.

'I won't be seeing her again.' Tom said, hanging his head in shame.

'Amigo, what you say...you have the real fights! What's about?'

'She took me back to her place. It...it was decorated like a martial arts DoJo. It was an ambush!'

'Mama Mia! Who is this Bastarda?' Carlo said, venom now colouring his voice. 'Tell me where I find her!'

'Let it go,' Tom pleaded, shocked by Carlo's need for action. He was embarrassed enough by being smash-dated let alone getting his housemate involved in a revenge mission. Besides, Carlo had only been in the country a month and this was the last thing he needed to get involved with.

'What you mean let it go? Carlo, he fix her up for you! What is her number?' Carlo insisted.

'I met her on the internet, remember?' Tom said, hoping this would put Carlo's vengeance into the too hard basket.

'What's the site?' Carlo probed, undeterred.

'It costs 500 bucks to join. Forget about it.'

'I pay FIVE THOUSAND DOLLARS to get square for you, amigo mio. The site?' Carlo demanded.

'LuvInc.com,' Tom said, folding. He anticipated Carlo's next question and added, 'Tricky_Nicky69.'

Carlo thought about that for a moment.

'Is a very funny name, no? But I still FIX HER UP FOR YOU!' Carlo assured Tom with a most convincing tone.

*****

It felt surreal for Chester to be standing out the front of his parish church on a weekday. There was only one other vehicle in the car park besides his van, and no mingling of Catholic devotees that were usually assembled there on Sunday mornings.

Chester entered the church and made his way to the front, dipping his fingers into holy water on the way and crossing himself humbly.

Extremely sombre, he walked slowly down the aisle to the altar and dropped coins into a collection box before picking up a fresh candle and lighting it using the flame of one that was already burning. He placed the candle into a holder, knelt, crossed himself once more and began to pray.

After ten minutes of concentrated prayer Chester heard the confessional open and close followed by the echoes of quick footsteps toward the rear of the church. Realising he was the next confessor up to bat he stood and made his way to the confessional, opened the door and took a seat.

After 10 seconds and what felt like an eternity Chester cleared his throat.

'Forgive me father for the sins I am about to commit.'

'Peace be with you my son,' was Father O'Leary's reply.

Chester noticed the priest was looking straight ahead.

'How long has it been since your last con—' Father O'Leary paused to readjust his question, then continued. 'Did you say sins you're *about* to commit?'

'That's correct, Father, about to,' Chester confirmed.

'My son, I cannot offer forgiveness for something you've not yet done. Tell me, what compels you to commit these sins?' he asked in a comforting tone.

Chester exhaled, looked down at his shoes and started at the beginning.

'Ten years ago my wife had a horse riding accident and as a result became paralysed from the waist down.'

'I see, my son. Go on.'

'She saw it as a sign from above and ever since then she won't consider her marriage duties. Not even once.'

Chester paused but was once again gently urged to continue by Father O'Leary's soft voice.

'I've been faithful to her since we fell in love but this past week I've been on a dating web site and forgive me, but I'm about to make up for the last ten years!'

'Did you make a date?' the priest questioned.

'No father, I've made five—Monday to Friday with five different women!'

Father O'Leary began to cough as if he had an orange stuck in his throat. He understood why Chester's guilt had led him to confession, but five women in a row? That was beyond overkill.

'Are you alright, Father?' Chester asked, thinking he was suffering from smoker's cough.

Father O'Leary took out his handkerchief and wiped heavy sweat away from his brow.

'Yes, I'm fine, my son. You did say five, correct?

'Yes, five,' Chester answered.

Father O'Leary thought carefully about his next question not wanting to give away that he was a little unconvinced by Chester's story.

'Perhaps they're just lonely, needing companionship?' he offered, giving Chester an opportunity to come back to reality.

'I have a poem from one,' Chester replied. 'I can read it to you if you like?'

'If you think it will give me a better understanding of their needs,' Father O'Leary replied.

'All things are equal, Monday's a date, We'll play hide and seek, Your nuts in my cake!'

This time Father O'Leary held back his cough. Realising Chester was truly in serious temptation territory this was the moment to lead his lost lamb back to the flock using all the skills his 40 years as a confidant had afforded him.

'You've lived an exemplary life, my son. Are you prepared for the consequences of your actions upon your soul?'

Chester felt his guilt rise again.

'Am I unforgivable?' he asked sadly.

'The fact you're here means God has not left or forsaken you. You're being tested, my son, and a great test it is too!' he concluded.

'Please help me, Father!' Chester begged.

Father O'Leary offered a saviour thanks to his disciplined study of the saints.

'Sunday is St Joseph's Day, the patron Saint of Fidelity,' he explained. 'I will light a candle and pray for you and your wife in the blessed Saint's name. But you must promise me action in return.'

The mention of St Joseph triggered something in Chester's memory. He was desperate to hear Father O'Leary's offer.

'Of course, yes, anything,' Chester beseeched.

'It is imperative, my son,' Father O'Leary continued, 'that you will try and rekindle that first love between you and your wife.'

'But I've tried everything,' Chester sobbed, a hint of frustration rising to the surface.

'Seek and ye shall find, knock and the door shall open,' said Father O'Leary with finality and resolution. 'Go in peace, my son.'

Chester crossed himself and exited the confessional.

—

'Peace be with you too, Father.'

CHAPTER XVII

WILL'S first official job as President of Luv Inc was transporting Abigail from his apartment to his office. His second was measuring, ordering and installing a new curtain so she could get the perfect balance of filtered sunlight in her tank. His third job was unexpected. He'd received a call from reception to alert him that there was a woman in the foyer, CV in hand, requesting a job interview. Will had her CV brought into him but he didn't get much further than her profile picture before he informed the receptionist to escort the applicant into his office.

To Will, Felicia Reardon was all numbers. A ripe 26 year old with, he guessed, a 34-25-34 figure and on a face appeal scale of one to knock out, she was a heavyweight champion. At one point during the interview he had to put her CV and references on his desk so she wouldn't notice his shaking hands. Even Abigail seemed a little excited by her presence.

'I'm very impressed, Miss Reardon,' he said, trying extremely hard to keep his eyes on hers.

'Thank you, Mr. Jackson, but please call me Flea,' she replied.

'Wow, you play bass guitar too?' was his ridiculous attempt at humour, but even so she giggled at the obvious reference to the Red Hot Chili Peppers musician.

'And you can call me Will. Welcome aboard Flea!'

'I got a job? Don't you want to contact my references first?' she asked, stunned.

'I don't think they're going to sing your praises any more than they've already written,' he assured her.

'I see why your company is going places; you don't fool around... So what will my position be?'

Will had quite a few positions in mind but was having trouble narrowing it down to just one.

'How about we discuss that over dinner?' he asked.

'I can't,' she said, 'I have must do plans tonight, sorry. How about you tell me all about yourself and Luv Inc now and perhaps we can find a position together?' Flea put a hand into her stylish LV handbag and retrieved her cell phone. She thumbed it into memo mode, hit record and put it on the table with a seductive smile. 'That's if you can spare even more time on me right now, of course.'

Will scoffed at the challenge. He index finger pointed her to the plaque on his desk.

'We got all the time in the world 'cause as you can see I'm the Prez!' he grinned. Flea responded with an intoxicating bimbo giggle that just seemed to encourage Will. 'Now, bring your seat over a little closer...'

ONE HOUR AND 32 MINUTES LATER...

Flea and her real boss Randall Stevens were in his office listening to the recording she'd made on her phone of Will recounting the Luv Inc story thus far, trying not to let the truckload of exaggerated bullshitting coming out of Will's mouth get in the way of the facts.

'Two days later, "WHAM" I got two thousand paid-up Luv Inc members and a million Suffering Succotash dollars in the bank!'

Flea couldn't stand the sound of Will's irritating voice any longer and unceremoniously hit the pause button on her phone.

'Can you believe how dumb this guy is?' she spat out in contempt.

'Dumb,' Randall echoed, deep in thought. 'His business just turned over in a week what we do in six months!' he said with appreciation and envy in his voice. Their conversation was interrupted by a knock at the door. 'Come in.'

Hacker walked in with a file in hand.

'Ze file you requested, Patron.' He passed the file to his boss.

'Hey there Hacker,' Flea chirped.

'Hallo, mon cherie, where have you been?' Hacker asked with excitement. He was always extra perky when Flea was around.

'You know, here, there, on special assignment,' she replied, causing Randall to shoot her a, "Be Quiet!" stare. Taking the hint she concluded the conversation. 'See you round the water fountain!'

After staring at her for a few more seconds Hacker realised they were waiting for him to leave, so he left quickly, bumping into the door on his way out and leaving them alone once again. Randall flicked through the paperwork he'd just received then paused when he came to one of the last pages.

'Bullseye!' he said, excitedly.

'What've you got?' Flea asked.

'It's not what I got, it's who,' Randall said, and passed her a copy of Luv Inc.'s lease agreement.

'Ravi Muhammad Ali,' she read out. 'Who's that?'

'That, my sweetness, is the name of Will's business partner and, I bet, the real brains behind Luv Inc!'

'I wonder why Will never mentioned him?' she said, disappointed that she hadn't extracted this information from Will herself.

'Because, my dear, he wanted to keep to himself your most scintillating lips, spectacular cleavage, and hypnotising eyes...and because he's "The Prez!"' Randall exclaimed before diving into a fit of laughter.

Calming down and coming back to the business at hand

Randall began to hatch a plan and tried to send it to Flea via E.S.P. by staring deeply into her eyes. Finally, he nodded with the hint of a smile playing on his lips.

'Tell me you're not thinking what I think you're —'

'That's exactly what you're going to do!' Randall breathed excitedly.

'But I can't stand another fifteen minutes with that imbecile,' Flea whined, but Randall continued, oblivious to her complaints.

'Form a wedge between Will and Ravi. Help Will drain the Luv Inc to its knees and leave the rest to me!' he continued, getting more and more excited.

Flea shook her head in disagreement but she knew from the resolute look on Randall's face that resistance was futile. She decided to leverage the outcome a little more in her favour.

'So...what's in it for moi?' she said, pointing to herself with both thumbs.

Randall knew the fetishes of his understudy. After all, she'd been in his shadow for eight years and had stuck with him during the slimmest times in the industry's history. He put a hand on a steel scale replica of his Porsche Cayman that took pride of place on his desk. Next, he took it for a spin with sound effects.

'Rum-Rumm-Rummmmmmmm,' he started then shifted into second gear, 'Rhurrrrrrrrrrrmmm!' he continued as he drove it over her fingers.

Flea resisted the temptation to smirk, wanting to push her deal into a higher gear.

'And?' she questioned, straight-faced.

Randall looked to his nearby bookshelf and spotted a globe. He retrieved it, spun it round, put it on the table then extended his arms like Superman in flight.

'And?' Flea continued to push, knowing her boss was well aware of how overdue she was for a first class holiday.

Randall needed a moment to think. He looked around his office then returned her stare, held up his palms, crossed his thumbs, then began to wiggle his fingers, gesticulating the story of Incy Wincy Spider.

'What the hell does that mean?' Flea asked, finally cracking her poker face.

'Think you could share an office with a Tarantula, Prez?' he asked.

Flea offered Randall her hand.

'Now that's a deal with legs.'

CHAPTER XVIII

DUE to the embarrassment of revealing his black eye story that morning, Tom had spent the workday soul-searching. When he arrived home Carlo was waiting for him and immediately sat him down to explain his revenge strategy. Tom agreed with Carlo's conclusion that the only way to fight fire was with fire, however, he was unsure about Carlo's plan to put Nicky's flame out.

On the other hand Carlo was excited by the adventure. He'd spent the day shopping for props and told Tom to wait in the lounge room while he retreated into his bedroom. After ten minutes he called out to Tom from his hiding spot in the hall.

'OK. You ready?' Carlo asked.

'Bring it on!' replied Tom.

'Ta-dah!' Carlo sprung into the lounge like a kangaroo and stood there, hands on hips as proud as punch.

'You look like a stalker,' Tom said, taking in each piece of Carlo's disguise.

He'd spent a pretty penny on spy quality facial hair, fake glasses and a wig. He'd also bought a complete 70s retro outfit that seemed to push his age from an early twenty-something to someone who looked thirty plus.

'What is a stalker?' Carlo asked, and then spun around like a Milan fashion model.

Tom avoided the question by asking one of his own.

'You sure you want to do this?'

'Don't try to change my mind!'

'I'm not. I'm just not sure about your disguise, that's all.' Tom replied.

'This Tricky Nicky, she lives in Brisbane, no?' Carlo questioned.

'True that,' said Tom.

'I'm a go to fix her up so good I no want her to see me on the street. Capish?'' Carlo answered, hoping his confidence would rub off onto Tom. 'Now take a good photo.'

Tom took out his cell phone and switched it into camera mode.

'Say cheese.'

FLASH! Carlo moved so Tom could capture another profile picture. FLASH! He put a hand onto a nearby doorframe and smiled. FLASH!

Happy with the photo session Carlo motioned Tom to follow him to his bedroom. Taking a seat at his computer Carlo connected the phone and downloaded the shots onto the screen. He maximised his Luv Inc profile page and clicked on the Upload Photo icon. Next, he typed in the numbers of his credit card and pressed enter. After thirty seconds a message confirmed that he was now able to access all of the member features on Luv Inc and wished him success on his journey to finding the partner he desired.

After high-fiving Carlo's palm Tom looked at the poster on the wall. It was written in Italian, an advertisement to come and train with Carlo, and showed him in full flight dressed in martial arts gear, complete with black belt. In bold print and highlighted at the bottom of the poster was its title: "Carlo de Luca: European Middle-Weight Kickboxing Champion."

*****

Later that evening Nicky opened a message from a contender with the profile name Looking4Kicks. She clicked on the message then sized up Carlo, AKA Georgio's photos. With the victory of pounding Tom still fresh in her mind she immediately hit reply and began to type.

'Looking for kicks, ey, Giorgio?' she chuckled to herself. 'Well, you've definitely come to the right girl.'

CHAPTER XIX

ALEX had been scheming a successful confrontation with her dad ever since arranging the date with Joan. In the process she'd lost her appetite and had to spend lunchtime in the school library as far away as possible from the smell of food. There, and in the pages of a psychology book, she'd found a potential solution to getting John to accept the date with minimal collateral damage. Theory, however, was one thing; practice, quite another.

Tonight, the second in a row of zero dinner, John asked if Alex was ill and even offered to take her to the family doctor. That was just the opening she was looking for. She made her father take a seat on the lounge while she went to her bedroom to retrieve the relevant items to help explain her disposition. She returned with pieces of A4 paper and her piggybank in hand.

'Daddy, I really need your opinion,' she said with a sombre tone.

'Sure, sweetie, what about?' he asked.

'Why are people so cruel to each other?'

Sensing the question as a discontentment regarding her deformity, John gently brushed the hair back from her face. For the first time in years he looked unhindered upon the red birthmark that consumed the left side of her face.

'Hurt people...hurt people, I guess,' he said.

Alex handed him an A4 print of Joan's profile picture. John looked into it, mesmerised by how close she came to being a clone of his beloved Grace.

'Who's this?' he asked.

'Do you think she's beautiful?'

'She…she's amazing,' John replied, still transfixed by her picture.

Without hesitation Alex opened and poured the contents of her piggybank into a pile at his feet.

'Do you know what this is?' she asked.

'What's up, little chicken?' John probed, genuinely concerned.

'This is every penny, dollar and treasure I've ever collected. And it's all yours!'

John searched his memory desperate to find a clue to the cause of her trauma.

'I don't want —' he started, before Alex cut him off.

'It's yours. Want to know why?' she asked, passion consuming her voice. She handed him copies of his Luv Inc profile and of Joan's messages. 'Can you read that one out please?' she said, pointing to one of Joan's messages.

John cleared his throat.

'Dear John, I feel like I've known you my whole life. Saturday cannot come fast enough. Truly yours, JO XXOO.' He looked at Alex. 'What's this?'

'Her name is Joan. She wants to meet you. But Daddy, there's something else.'

Alex put a hand into her pocket retrieving his missing credit card and giving it back to him. 'I had to steal this to pay for your membership. I'm sorry,' she said, looking down into her lap.

John stared at her, lost for words. He looked at Joan's profile, picture, and messages, down to the piggybank booty on the floor, and then back to his daughter.

'Do you understand what you've done?' he asked her, his voice soft and full of emotion.

Alex nodded.

'Oh no you don't,' he said, his voice suddenly going hard.

He held up Joan's photo for Alex to inspect. 'You see her?' he asked.

Alex answered with a nod once again.

'That's about how old you're going to be when your grounding finishes!'

Alex noticed how his rage opened his eyes wide and started to beg.

'Daddy, please don't get —' but it was too late.

'Dancing classes! Internet! Hip-Hop music! Banana split ice cream! Say goodbye to them because they're ALL HISTORY!' he shouted.

Alex was in deeper trouble territory than she'd ever been before. She did, however, have one last card to play.

'You don't even want to understand WHY?' she rallied.

'WHY, WHAT?' John yelled at the top of his voice.

'I just want a friend, too!' she yelled back, then ran to her room and slammed the door shut behind her.

Angry with himself for raising his voice so venomously, John slid to his knees in disappointment. Something in the pile of loot on the floor grabbed his attention. Transfixed, he stretched out his hand and retrieved an item he'd thought had been lost forever. An antique locket he'd given to Grace on Valentine's Day.

Transformed back through time and space he opened the locket to see if what she'd put inside the frame had also survived.

Tears welled in his eyes as he gazed upon the cheek-to-cheek photo of them taken while they were snuggled together inside a $2 photo booth. Through his tears he focussed upon the inscription engraved onto the other half of the cover—FRIENDS FOREVER.

Now understanding what Alex meant by describing the contents of her piggybank as containing treasures his tears, like hot-running wax, streamed from his chin down onto the locket, splashing onto the rest of her treasures below.

After a few minutes John considered Alex's statement from the other evening. "What about me?" she had said. "What about me?" He finally grasped the full ramifications of her question and how he had to answer to it.

John scooped up the miscellaneous treasure from the carpet back into Alex's piggybank. He affixed its rubber stopper in place on its belly then got up and made his way to his study. He took out a piece of his finest writing paper and his favourite pen and scribed what he considered one of the most important documents of his life. He folded and inserted it into the coin gap of Alex's piggybank then exited his study to plant it where she couldn't help but find it. He went to his bedroom and set his alarm an hour earlier so that he'd be long gone before Alex awoke and discovered it.

Just minutes ago Alex had cried herself to sleep but not before spending a long time looking at herself in the mirror and contemplating the countless times her heinous birthmark had infected potential friendships thus far in her short life. She had also been tempted to email Joan and to inform her that Saturday night was off but concluded that if her dad came in unexpectedly and caught her mid email there was no telling how the real John_007 would have completed it.

The next morning Alex was awakened by the sound of her father's car starting up and pulling away. She lay in bed for a while relieved she had the whole house to herself. When Alex

—

finally got out of bed she exited her room on the way to the shower, but as she stepped into the hall she stubbed her big toe on her piggybank, knocking her treasure chest over. She picked it up and was about to throw it at the wall in anger when she spotted a note sticking out of the coin slot. She unfolded it.

Alex,
I've changed my mind. I'll go on the date.
Love Dad.
PS. See you tonight xo.

Alex's celebration dance made the coins and treasure in her piggybank jingle. *What a relief,* she thought. She jingled back to her bedroom and threw her piggybank onto her bed then skipped to her desk. She opened the Luv Inc page on her laptop then started the process of redeeming a babysitting voucher.

After clicking Submit, Alex went into John's room and started through his wardrobe on a mission to choose the perfect outfit for his date. It was here as she sorted through his tired shirts and pants that she realised he hadn't bought any fashionable new clothes for over a year. *I'll have to personally attend to this,* she thought, and the only opportunity to go shopping together would be sometime this Saturday. She left his room to prepare for school, counting down the hours and minutes until she could manoeuvre him to her favourite shopping mall for a deluxe head-to-toe makeover.

CHAPTER XX

CELENE always made her daily call to Ravi just before lunch to confirm the overnight membership figures and other executive business matters. She had another vital job to cross off her list before calling him: to confirm a babysitter for Saturday night for John_007. Celene enjoyed talking to the executive from their babysitting service, People Power, who handled the Luv Inc account.

Rene also enjoyed her conversations with Celene. While the babysitting side of her parents' company was initially only a small concern, due to Luv Inc.'s members' insatiable appetite to use their free babysitting benefits, it was rapidly outgrowing their staff roster.

Rene heard Celene's incoming call through her headset and smiled.

'Good afternoon People Power, this is Rene.'

'Hi Rene, it's Celene from Luv Inc. How are you?'

'I'm well! It's nice to hear your voice again, Celene. How can I help today?' Rene asked, with genuine zest.

'I need another sitter for Saturday night,' Celene said.

'Can you hold, Celene, I'll have to double check with the boss?'

'Sure thing,' Celene replied.

Rene put Celene on hold and pressed a button that connected her to her mum, and boss, Kara.

'Mum, I have Celene from Luv Inc on the phone looking for another sitter for Saturday night. How's the roster looking?' She could hear her mum tapping on the keyboard of her computer through her headphones as she waited for Kara to confirm or deny.

'I have one girl available and one on stand-by but I think

the standby's going to be booked for the Hanson job,' Kara answered.

'Thanks, Mum,' Rene said and switched back to her call with Celene.

'You're in luck! We have a girl available but I'll need confirmation no later than close of business this afternoon.'

'You're a lifesaver, Rene! Lock her in for 7pm Saturday. I'll email you the address and confirmation shortly.'

'Always a pleasure talking with you, Celene,' said Rene.

'Likewise Rene. Talk soon.' Celene ended her call with Rene and then called her Luv Inc client to confirm the babysitting appointment for this weekend.

John was taking an office break and strolling around the Brisbane City streets when he received the call from Celene.

'Hi, John, this is Celene from Luv Inc. I'm calling to —' before she could finish she was cut off.

'I'm sorry, you're from where?' John questioned, slightly bewildered.

'LuvInc.com,' Celene replied.

'What is LuvInc.com?' John asked.

'We're an internet dating service of which you are a member,' she reminded him.

The lights suddenly came on and John switched into executive mode, pressing the phone to his ear.

'Yes, of course I know who you are. Forgive me, I'm a little new to all this. What can I do for you Celene?'

'I received your email this morning and your application's been approved and confirmed,' she said.

'Look, it's been a busy morning, could you remind me

again what I've applied for?' John asked, knowing that since he was a client she'd have to play the game.

'A babysitter for your first date on Saturday night,' she reminded him.

'Ahhh, that email. Yes, of course. Now, remind me, do I have to pay cash or are you happy to take my credit card details?' John asked.

'Neither—it's part of your membership benefits. The sitter will be at your house at 7pm sharp. And John? Good-luck on your date.'

'Thank you. Goodbye,' he said, as he hung up the phone with a huge sigh of relief.

Celene hung up then looked around the office just in time to notice Will and Flea enter the office floor then disappear into Martin Truman's cubicle. They reappeared and entered Seth's cubicle then, without notice, Will was in front of her with Flea at his side.

'Meeting in the boardroom in 5,' Will relayed.

'Will Ravi be joining us?' she asked.

'Won't be necessary. Make sure you bring your pad and a pen, you've a lot of work to get onto,' he replied.

As they marched off Celene followed them with her eyes. Halfway to the boardroom Flea turned her head back around and gave Celene a smirk that made her "Bitch" alarm go off. Celene got out of her chair and visited the cubicle next to hers.

'Sorry, Seth, quick question: Who is that woman who just walked in with Will?' she asked.

'Not sure, but she's definitely not the gardener,' he jested.

'Thanks,' she replied, knowing she should have thought twice about asking the young punk on the block.

Celene got back to her cubicle to send the promised email off to Rene. Next, she picked up her notepad and pen and began the migration to the boardroom with Seth, Martin Truman and new company secretary, Elaine, who led the charge with a bundle of paperwork in her hands. Once inside

Elaine put the stack of papers in front of Flea who was standing over Will, who was already seated in the director's chair at the head of the board table.

'Please come in and sit down,' Flea motioned to everyone.

Celene took a seat to Will's left as far away as possible from Flea. Once they were all seated Flea spoke to Elaine as if she were in charge.

'Thank you, dear. That will be all.'

Who is this person? Celene thought to herself as she put up her guard even more.

Flea proceeded to strut around the boardroom dropping the executive memos onto the table in front of each of them. Though Celene's eyes focussed on her memo her mind was preoccupied with searching for the name of the perfume Flea was wearing. *That's it!* she recalled, as it brought back memories of a $1,500 an ounce scent at the duty free shop. It was odd that its price came to her before its name: Hermes 24 Faubourg. She looked up and caught Flea returning her stare.

'Its come to my attention that although we're looking good on paper some things need to be addressed,' began Will. 'Firstly, our membership fee: it's too high and needs to shrink.' Will looked to his team for support. *If it's not broken why try and fix it*, thought Celene. To date, not one Luv Inc client she'd come across had complained about the membership fee.

'We've set an industry standard here, Will—the benefits are second to none! In fact, I've nearly booked out our babysitting agency with jobs for this weekend!' Celene protested.

Will used her volley to continue.

'Thanks for bringing me to item two, Celene: Benefits. Free condoms? Discounts at cinemas and restaurants? Hell, if you can't afford rubbers, a movie, or a meal you shouldn't be dating!' he said with contempt.

Martin Truman looked at Celene in disbelief. She raised an eyebrow to him to speak up. Martin turned his attention to Will.

'Feedback from our clients indicates that our member benefits are our point of difference from every other site on the market!' he proclaimed.

'I don't care what our punters have to say, cut them all off!' Will demanded.

For the next minute Celene didn't hear anything Will or anyone else in the boardroom had to say. Her mind flashed back to that moment when she began to appreciate the genuine inter-relational public needs their online service provided. This factor was what she'd needed to give her heart and soul — and not just her expertise — to this vital work. She'd also started to see how effectively her input, especially in the referral and converting of follow-up members, was getting high percentage results. She couldn't help but take Will's, and Flea's, attacks and bitchiness to her work personally. Once again she thought, *Where is Ravi? Got to speak to Ravi!* Her daydreaming stopped just as Will highlighted another item from the memo.

'The other big news is that Luv Inc is going to stage a huge, no-expense-spared party for female members only!' he confirmed, the self satisfied grin on his face mirrored and echoed in the sentiments of his equally testosterone-injected colleague.

'Alright!' Seth shouted in triumph, and began panting like a puppy.

'You've hired out The Mansion?' Celene said apprehensively, looking up from her memo.

The Mansion, as its name hinted, was Brisbane's answer to the Playboy Bosses' original swinging 50s residence which was located at 1340 North State Parkway, Chicago. It was available for functions and bachelor party hire with a starting price tag of $40,000 per night. All this depended on the extra accessories hirers wanted to scratch their itch. It was way out of the league of anyone Seth or his mates knew. This was the reason for his above the sound barrier response.

'It so suits Will's profile as the rising star of Brisbane's Internet King Pins, don't you think?' Flea said, attempting to justify the lavish proposal.

Celene let go of her inner composure and opened fire.

'Excuse me, but exactly who the fuck are you?' she glared at Flea, and with the venom in her tone instantly turned the boardroom into a freezer.

After seconds that appeared to drag on for hours Seth slid down his chair like a greased monkey. Martin let out a "Whoa" under his breath as Celene continued to stare Flea down. Speechless, Flea gave Will a shin kick from under the table.

'A-Hum....Flea...is...my PA.' Will cleared his throat some more.

Celene's gaze ricocheted from Flea's exposed, over-abundant cleavage, back to her eyeball-to-eyeball death stare.

'More like T'n'A, if you ask me,' she stated distastefully.

'HOW DARE YOU!' Flea fired back with a roar as if calling on the Gods of morality to defend her honour.

Celene chuckled, amused by Flea's unconvincing attempt at being offended. She stood up to leave.

'I didn't jump on board Luv Inc to turn it into a sleazy, all "promise-but-no-delivery" bordello! Before I do anything I'm talking to Ravi and I suggest the rest of you do the same!' She picked up her pad, pen, and executive memos and began to exit.

'You'll do as you're told or you're fired!' Will shouted after her, as Flea's pointy stiletto again came into violent contact with his shin. He hoped it was the bravado response she wanted.

Celene stopped in her tracks and turned around, livid.

'Neither you, nor Miss T'n'A hired me so I'd suggest reading the separation clause in my contract before you threaten me with anything!' She continued heading for the door.

'Should I remind you that it's Will who signs your pay cheques?' Flea said smugly. She couldn't resist getting a shot in herself.

Again, Celene stopped in her tracks and turned around, but this time she directed her response directly at Flea.

'I didn't know that but it does answer some quite obvious questions, don't you think?' she said with finality before storming out.

After an uncomfortable stillness it was Flea who broke the deafening silence caused by Celene's departure.

'Seth, I need you create an e-flyer for the Mansion Party and mass email it to every female member of Luv Inc. Think you can handle that?'

Once again Seth summed up his entire disposition with a single word.

'Alright.'

*****

Ravi was in a meeting with the state manager of a popular cinema chain, finalising the details of the Luv Inc discount movie offer deal, when he received a call from Celene. He excused himself before accepting the call.

'Hello, Celene. I'm in a meeting. I'll call you back as soon as I'm finished, OK?'

'Sure Ravi. How long?' she asked.

'Give me 15 minutes,' he answered.

Celene packed a few of her more important personal items from her workstation into her handbag, and left Luv Inc immediately. She drove to a nearby snack bar, parked, and went inside to get a cool drink to calm down her now torrential emotions. As she sat there sipping an ice tea she retrieved the executive memo from her handbag concluding it was something better seen with Ravi's eyes than explained over the phone. As promised, Ravi returned her call on time.

'Hello, Celene, what can I do for you?' he asked politely.

'I have to see you ASAP, Ravi. I think Will's going to destroy Luv Inc!' she said, the urgency evident in her voice.

'What? I can be there in half an hou—'

'I'm not at the office,' Celene said, cutting him off before continuing, 'I walked out.' She could just barely hold back her anger.

'I...I don't understand?' Ravi stuttered.

'Where are you? Perhaps we can meet half way?' she asked.

Ravi gave her an address for a trendy café in Paddington.

'I know it,' she replied. 'I'll see you soon.'

'I don't believe it,' Celene said, now face to face with Ravi and sipping a flat white coffee in the middle of the Paddington café.

Ravi had no choice but to explain the whole story of Luv Inc to Celene, from college conception to executive execution, after she'd detailed the minutes of the meeting and showed him the memo that was now crumpled up on the table.

'So you have absolutely no control whatsoever?' she questioned, wishing that all hope was not lost, but knowing otherwise.

'Of course I have some, but it is restricted,' he replied.

'I think we need a second opinion,' she stated firmly.

'What do mean?'

'Surely your lawyer left a legal remedy in the contracts, just in case something like this happened?' she probed.

Ravi could see why Celene had already ascended to the corporate heights achieved before her employment at Luv Inc. Her understanding of business law and the framework of company politics made him feel at ease when discussing his most sensitive Luv Inc information. *If only she were my business partner*, he thought.

'Perhaps, but I'll have to ask them,' Ravi replied.

'Who are "them"?' Celene asked.

Ravi dove into his briefcase and retrieved Michael Sachs' and Fred Gower's business cards and passed them to Celene. She studied them for a minute.

'Boy you don't muck around, Ravi. These are both big hitters. How'd you get onto them?' she asked.

'That's not important; but why you need to know, is.'

'Well, I don't really. Can you set up a conference so we can go through your contracts with them?' she asked.

Ravi took his time in responding, not because he didn't know Celene's suggestion was spot on but mainly because he was a little embarrassed he hadn't suggested it. He put his hand out for Celene to return the cards. Focussing on one, he took out his mobile and dialled.

'Yes, hello this is Ravi Ali. I am wanting to speak to Michael Sachs, please. I am his client.' He looked up to Celene who smiled in encouragement. He was glad she was on his side.

Seth was having a ball configuring his newest assignment. He'd already clicked and downloaded the many backgrounds for the e-flyer from the official Mansion website. Since this was a Luv Inc female party he had to stick to finding pictures of shirtless male waiters with bow ties and cheesy smiles rather than the usual ones he looked for—Playgirl Bunnies with big, bright futures in front of them. He photoshopped the images he found over a great image of the Mansion's outdoor function area and typed the kicker into the text box below: FREE CHAMPAGNE.

He then clicked and pasted the door prize into the flyer: a brand new red Alfa Romeo convertible that had been paid for, in cash, by Flea and Will before they had arrived at the office that morning. Flea also wanted, "FREE FOR ALL FEMALE LUVINC.COM MEMBERS—PARTY STARTS AT 8 SO DON'T BE LATE!" written onto the flyer, and although it was tacky, Seth thought Flea's RSVP option was somewhat applicable: "RSVP by emailing 'AVAILABLE' to party@luvinc.com." Pleased with his genius, Seth hit the Render Project icon.

'Three minutes, screw that,' he said in response to his computer's stopwatch estimation to complete the e-flyer

render. Instead of waiting at his desk Seth took off from his cubicle, went through the door of a nearby fire exit down the stairs and into the basement car park. He strolled to a spot near the rear of the building, put a hand into his pocket to find the three paper spliff he usually reserved for the afternoon walk to his train stop, lit it and took a toke that would have made Bob Marley proud. With his free hand, Seth thumbed autodial on his mobile, a call that was answered in two seconds flat.

'Hey, Seth, what's doin?' his mate Jeremy asked.

'You're not going to believe this, dude. Luv Inc is throwing a free-for-all-female-member-party at the Mansion, man!' Seth exclaimed.

'Bullshit! When?' Jeremy asked.

'Next Saturday night.'

'That's a bit short notice, Groover,' Jeremy asked.

'You shitting me! I'll be sending invitations out tonight and I'd be surprised if there'll be any vacancies left by the morning,' Seth said, then took another lung-buster toke.

'Can you get me in?' Jeremy asked.

Seth knew he would ask, thus the reason for his call. He blew enough smoke out for Houdini to hide an elephant behind before he replied.

'That depends?' Seth teased.

'What on?' Jeremy asked again.

'On whether or not you've been to the farm lately,' Seth replied, in their co-authorised drug code.

'Since when has my cupboard been like ol' Mother Hubbard's?' Jeremy replied.

They both broke into laughter.

'Well consider yourself officially invited then. Later, man,' Seth concluded. He stubbed out the last of his joint then dashed up the fire exit stairs, through the office, and back to his desk.

'Beauty,' he said to himself at his computer's confirmation that the flyer was all rendered and ready to go.

He thought he'd kill two birds with one stone and send the e-flyer to Flea firstly for her approval and secondly to confirm it would make the journey through cyber space. He attached it to an email and hit Send.

Seth got up to go to Will's office for a thumbs-up, but more importantly than receiving confirmation from Flea—who he knew would be in Will's office as per usual—was the fact that he was finally going to cross a Mansion "Par-tay" off his bachelor's must-do list. With an ounce of Jeremy's bush-weed confirmed he knew he'd arrive hi, high, hi-there! He knocked on the President's door and waited. Finally, he heard a muffled answer he assumed told him to come in and opened the door to find Will behind his desk.

'Sorry to bother you, Will, but is Flea around? Seth asked, now sensing that the THC from the joint was starting to short-circuit his reality.

Will responded by pointing past his shoulder to Flea who was at the other end of the office feeding Abigail her lunch with a pair of wooden chopsticks.

'Hi, Seth, what can I do for you?' she asked.

Seth made his way closer to Abigail's tank.

'I just wanted to let you know that I've finished the flyer and emailed it to you,' Seth said, now in close viewing proximity of Abigail's extraordinary culinary equipment.

'That was quick,' Flea replied, as Abigail loaded what

looked like a miniscule piece of road kill past her fangs and into her mouth. Flea smiled at Seth, amused by the concentrated look on his face. Recognising the cause of the redness in his eyes she played the situation a little further.

'Here, you give it a go,' she said, offering him the chopsticks.

This close encounter of witnessing a 20-centimetre tarantula during feeding time started to spin Seth's memory into the surreal bar scene from "Fear And Loathing In Las Vegas!" Almost as if on cue, Abigail startled and changed the direction of her attention directly to Seth.

'Me thinks to pass thanks,' Seth said. 'Take a peek at your inbox and email me your thoughts on the flyer,' he finished and then reversed back out the door.

Will waited until he was out of potential earshot.

'He's a weird one!'

'Perhaps...but aren't you all?' Flea retorted.

'What makes you think that?' Will asked.

'Open my email, will you, pet,' Flea said to him, avoiding his question. 'Let's see if he's captured the Luv Inc verve for your Coming Out Party, shall we?' she asked, putting the chopsticks down and making her way to Will's desk.

'The what of Luv Inc?' Will questioned.

Flea bent over to whisper into his ear.

'The verve, Will; the very essence of your presence,' she said with a Monroe-like husky tone, and took a seat on his lap.

Will gulped then fumbled for his keypad.

'This Mansion party is the most brilliant thing that's ever happened to me!' he stated as he pressed the keys on his keypad.

'Ditto,' she whispered and put an arm around Will's neck as they waited for his computer screen to boot-up.

*****

In a plush boardroom office 20 floors above Brisbane's city district Celene was in polished oak wood heaven. She was sitting around the largest conference room table she'd ever seen with Gower, Sachs, and Ravi who was most impressed that they'd cleared their afternoon schedules to attend to this urgent meeting.

Ravi and Celene had already spent 10 minutes filling them in on the current status quo of Luv Inc, including the fact that Will considered Ravi's input into the company all but mute and about the instigation of the free party of a lifetime at the Mansion.

'From a legal perspective Will's holding most of the aces,' Sachs said, after first laying down the ground rules of their talks. Why? Well, since Will was also their client and the president and biggest stakeholder in Luv Inc, it was professionally most inappropriate that he was not invited.

'We've created an uncontrollable monster,' Ravi said, cracking and finally showing emotion in front of Celene for the first time.

'You still have two hundred and sixty-five thousand in the kitty; surely he's not stupid — correction — un-savvy enough to flush those kind of reserves away?' Gower questioned.

Celene felt the vibration on her phone. She touched the screen and noticed it was an email, its sender none other than the man at the centre of this meeting, and president of Luv Inc, William Jackson. Knowing it was unprofessional to be seen opening it in the meeting she sneaked her phone under the table, opened the email and downloaded the attachment to discover the poster for the Mansion party with all the added extras she'd missed due to her early exit from this morning's meeting. She looked up as Ravi continued.

'He's lowering the membership fee and taking away all the benefits. On top of that he has booked the Mansion for a free-for-all-single-women-party!'

Celene noticed Sachs and Gower give each other a, '"What's wrong with that?" or a, "Hope we're invited!" look. She had to bring them all back to earth and get them up to speed on the extravagance of Will's actions.

'The Mansion is 40 grand a night, the door prize another 30, add to that the free champagne, entertainment, food and catering staff and you can kiss another 70 or 80 grand goodbye,' she contributed to the debate for the first time. She could see Gower going over the sums in his head.

'That still leaves you with a hundred and forty thousand. I can't see him getting through all those reserves,' Gower insisted.

Ravi couldn't believe his ears. Then it hit him — the biggest threat to the whole Luv Inc enterprise came to him. What was even worse was that it was his original idea; he had no choice but to declare it publicly.

'Luv Inc has a 30 day 100% money back guarantee,' he said slowly and carefully. They were all listening now. 'If for some reason the loss of benefits or maybe a reaction to the punch at the party upsets them, well...do the math. We are in a very, very critical and vulnerable situation, my friends.'

Rene noticed Gower going into mental overdrive doing the calculations. It was Sachs who finally offered a legal perspective.

'There are dozens of ways to stall that from happening, Ravi. Trust me,' he assured, 'I can give that conclusion so much red tape that before they see 1 cent they'll think they're resigning from the CIA!'

'That's not the point, Mr. Sachs. I am an honest man and what I've promised is what I want to deliver,' Ravi insisted, resolute in his decision. 'Just today I've negotiated a deal with a major cinema chain giving our clients 40% off all cinema tickets. How do you think I am going to feel having to cancel the offer even before we have a chance to apply it?

The integrity of this statement really hit a cord with Celene reaffirming that for both her and Ravi this was not about money: it was just about being straight shooters.

'I see your position, Ravi, and I honour your morals,' Sachs said, 'but we can't confront Will without letting him know that this meeting has taken place. You're just going to have to bite the bullet and do the dirty work in talking him out of it.'

'I'm afraid that time has passed,' Celene butted in, holding out her phone to show them the email. 'The flyer has already hit 300 inboxes and counting,' she concluded.

Ravi took the phone from her to see it in more detail and then hung his head.

'Ravi, there's no point accepting defeat before you've even stepped into the ring,' Gower pointed out. 'Have a little faith that you can make him see reason.'

'Gentleman, we appreciate your time. I'll keep you informed if we have any success,' Ravi said, without a hint of victory in his voice.

At that moment something stirred in Celene's photographic memory about Flea. *Where have I seen her before?* she asked herself once more, trying to again figure out how she knew this evil woman. As much as she enjoyed the plush surroundings she was now anxious to get out of there ASAP and solve this question that had been lying at the edge of her mind since they had first met. She also had a gut feeling that once she found this answer it would solve so many more of their questions. And her gut feelings were pretty much always spot on.

CHAPTER XXI

NICKY had been counting the clock down to Friday knock-off all afternoon. She'd tasted "Man-Blood" through Tom and the anticipation of reproducing that on Georgio was whipping up the same adrenaline infused sensations she'd only experienced before at a karate tournament. There was a slight downside in the form of the guilt she was feeling from the lies she had to tell her girlfriend and Sensei, Kate, to free herself up tonight for her date. The guilt, however, was only simmering on the furthest back burner in her subconscious, so she was able to push it away as she stood freshly dried and naked in her walk-in wardrobe searching for the irresistible outfit that would lure her next target back to her den of Zen and iniquity.

On the other side of the city Carlo and Tom were synchronizing the night's events with military precision. Nicky had again requested a rendezvous at the exact same Subway restaurant where she'd hooked up with Peeping Tom. Carlo had digested Tricky Nicky's modus operandi word for word as Tom described it in detail.

'OK, so once inside she's going to order a Footlong and have it cut in half,' Tom relayed.

'What is "Foot Long?"' Carlo questioned, oblivious to the menu item.

'It's a bread roll about a foot long,' Tom answered. 'Anyway. Once you're at the table she's not going to eat anything while staring at you like you're a hot fudge sundae,' he reported. 'It's then that she's going to try and get you back to her place for dessert!'

Carlo was quite amused by all these Tricky Nicky facts but kept it to himself knowing they'd deflate Tom's feelings: he'd been hurt enough by being laid out instead of getting laid on his date with Nicky. Carlo actually admired Nicky's stealth and cunning, however, none of this was going to stop him teaching her a lesson she'd never forget.

'So, as soon as you're finished,' Tom continued, 'I'll be waiting for you in the car, passenger door open and engine running,' he concluded, a smile of satisfied delight now on his face.

'Is good plan, Tom,' Carlo concurred. 'I promise I fix her up real good for you!' They slapped palms and patted each other on the back.

15 minutes later Tom dropped a fully outfitted Carlo, dressed like a 70s retro fashion victim complete with fake moustache, wig, side-burns, beard, and coke-bottle glasses two streets behind the Subway restaurant. He strolled around the corner and to his surprise spotted Nicky at the entrance waiting for him. His adrenaline started to pump as he prepared to present himself to her as Georgio, the ass-kicker from somewhere in Italy. Nicky looked in his direction and offered him a smile.

My God, what a bombshell, Carlo thought, as he took in her ensemble—a skin-tight electric blue outfit that highlighted her muscular and full figure. Her handbag was a dark-toned leather that matched her brown eyes, rare for someone with naturally blonde hair. Being down wind, he also took in her scent: he recognised it as Angel. *What a paradox*, he thought, and he replaced the picture of beauty in front of him with one of Tom's black eye to keep himself true to the mission at hand.

'Giorgio?' she asked.

'Tricky?' Carlo replied, and returned her smile.

'It's Nicky, not Tricky,' she answered with a giggle.

'So sorry, Nicky, my English is a little confuse when I reads,' he said, taking the piss.

'That's OK,' she said, 'you hungry?'

Carlo looked inside the restaurant and saw the pictures on the wall of New York subway maps and train lines.

'Yes, but I no like the train food,' he answered.

'Train food?' Nicky asked; then the penny dropped. 'Subway's not like train food,' she said laughing.

'I no like even the trains, he make a me sick. Why no we get a pizza?' he suggested to test her resolve.

'You're funny! Come on, let's share a Footlong,' she asserted, taking him by the arm and leading him inside.

A few minutes later they were seated across from each other in a booth. Carlo was actually starving and attacked his half of the Footlong like a ferocious beast who hadn't seen a meal since the last full moon.

After devouring it he looked up and noticed she hadn't even touched her half. He pointed to it questioningly and Nicky shook her head, so he picked it up and started into it with the same beastly approach.

'I really like the train food, it's a very fresh-spicy, no?' he said contentedly when he finally came up for air. Nicky smiled not sure if this was a man or an eating machine. After swallowing, he spoke again. 'So why you no eats, no hungry?'

Nicky chose her response very carefully.

'I have an appetite alright, just not for food,' she said then waved him closer to whisper into his ear. 'I want to squeeze enough juice out of you to make an Italian-meringue pie!'

She leaned back into the booth expecting his eyes to pop out of their sockets

Carlo simply shrugged then continued munching the last of his six-inch before wiping his hands with a serviette. Finally, he leaned forward and waived her closer.

'I so sorry. I must tell you, Tricky, but Giorgio's papa teach him to only be the true gentleman. He never takes the woman to the bed on the first time!'

After a moment of eyeballing Nicky responded by kicking off her shoe and extending her leg, placing her foot between his crotch while her flexed big toe made little circles over his sack of spuds. As she expected it didn't take long for the doe to rise and the situation to progress from a big toe to a full foot massage. Carlo closed his eyes in bliss then re-opened them to find Nicky biting her lip, stroking her right nipple, and eyeing him with a lustful gaze more potent than the fangs of a cobra.

'OK, Tricky, for you I break my papa's words. But only if you beg Georgio like da pussycat,' Carlo said, pushing for an extra insult in addition to her forthcoming injury.

Nicky withdrew her foot then brought her bent hands to her face to simulate paws. She started licking them sensuously.

'Meowwww…meowwww…purrrr…purrrrrrrr…'

'Mamma mia, I think is time for the desserts!' Carlo responded, now definitely in the mood.

Nicky grinned then with gusto grabbed both her handbag and Carlo's hand on a mission out the door to their last course for the night.

As Nicky and Carlo rounded the corner into her street Carlo noticed Tom's car parked under a tree on the other side of the road, but there was no sign of Tom. Carlo guessed he'd slid down his seat at the sight of the car's headlights. They entered the driveway to her one story apartment complex and she halted in front of her garage door and asked him to get out to open it, a request that he as a gentleman was happy to accommodate. She parked, jumped out, then took Carlo by the hand and led him up a set of stairs and into her apartment.

Nicky opened the door and switched on a hall light before waving him inside, an act he acknowledged with a bow of his head. Once inside Carlo realised that Tom's descriptions of this suburban Dojo were an identical match right down to the wall timer and fighting mat. Carlo looked through the large glass doors over a small balcony but he couldn't see Tom anywhere. Behind him he heard Nicky plonk her handbag and keys onto the kitchen bench then the clomp-clomp of her shoes hitting the tiled floor. Carlo gave a thumbs-up to signal Tom that it was on, hoping that he could see him from wherever he was watching outside, then took his shoes off and stationed them neatly together in front of the glass doors. He walked into the centre of the fighting mat then turned square on to face Nicky.

'Is like a one big beds!' he said in jest, then asked, 'Why you have no TV?'

Nicky avoided his question by asking one of her own,

'So what style do you learn?' Then proceeded to size him up for a first assault.

'The kickboxing, like I say on my profile, no,' he answered.

'Ahhhh, you took your shoes off—you have respect for the mat,' she retorted.

'I see this in the movies. So what fights you know?' he prodded.

'A little kickboxing, but mostly karate. You want to spar?'

'Where you keeps the spa in such small apartment?' Carlo asked, playing dumb once again. This amused Nicky, yet he could tell her laugh was fake.

'Not a spa,' she said. She put up her guard: 'SPAR!' Nicky walked onto the mat and hit the wall clock. Carlo chuckled both at her stickling to her routine as described by Tom, and her presumption that she could match his skills.

'I no like to hits a woman, is very un-romantico, no?' he asked, as Nicky started to circle him, her guard up and ready.

'Well, maybe this woman . . . she wants to KICK YOUR FUCKING ASS! KEE-JAH.' Nicky performed a textbook perfect roundhouse kick to Carlo's head; he caught her leg a few inches from his face. With her limb still in his tight grip he leg swept Nicky ass first onto the mat. As she stared up at him a little dazed Carlo unbuttoned his shirt and threw it onto the kitchen counter. He turned back to her and witnessed her snap-spring to her feet. He began to circle her as she shaped up to him again.

'Lucky Bastard!' she hissed as she searched for his weak point.

'There is no lucky in karate, Tricky!' he said, knowing it would piss her off, but that was the whole point.

'The name is NICKY! HA-CHE!' she yelled, then dummied a right, then left kick, spun around with an outstretched arm and slapped him flush on the cheek, knocking his glasses into the corner, and his beard and one of his sideburns onto the floor. Nicky was pleased with herself but of course she knew something very fishy was at play here. 'Well, well, look who's the Tricky now?' she said to Carlo as he rubbed the sting out of his chin. 'So who sent you to me? Kate?'

Not waiting for a response Nicky charged at him again throwing one, two, three punches which Carlo blocked and side-stepped; he then put her into a clinch from behind. Nicky used all the strength her legs could muster, forcing his grip to loosen as she drove him backwards making him collide with the brick lounge room wall just under her clock and knocking the wind out of him.

Carlo took hold of the back of her blouse then pushed her forward ripping it off her and leaving her to stand in the middle of the mat in her bra and skirt.

'I ASKED YOU A QUESTION!' she screamed.

'I gives you the clue,' Carlo said, keeping an eagle eye on her as she continued circling him. 'Winner get to cum first!' he 'fessed up with a chuckle.

Nicky took a moment to register.

'Ah, yes! Peeping Tom! So how's his eye?' she asked with a smirk. Not waiting for his reply Nicky advanced again attempting to front kick Carlo in the guts, a move he countered with a two handed block, once again putting her into a clinch. Helpless, Nicky looked at their reflection from the glass doors as Carlo undid the clip at the back of her skirt. She elbowed him in the guts causing him to let her go. Her skirt slipped to the floor and she angrily kicked it away, now standing in the centre of the mat in only her underwear.

Across the road Tom got an eyeful of her hot curves and then a flash of her muscular butt and frilly G-string from his vantage point in the bottom branches of the tree across the road. He punched the air in victory.

'That's my man! Kick her ass!' he applauded.

Nicky watched on as Carlo, not to be outdone, unzipped and ripped his pants off and threw them to the floor. At that moment something clicked in her as she stared at his magnificent physique, this statue of David's hairless body except for a thin snail trail of fluff from his belly button to the inside of his bulging briefs.

Nicky started to feel a warmth between her thighs, something a male had not overwhelmed her with since leaving her small country town behind 18 months ago. Fighting that memory she advanced toward Carlo with another front kick that Carlo again blocked. He put her into another clinch from behind but she caught his leg, throwing him off balance and they fell into a heap on the mat.

Carlo pushed her chest-first into the canvas and saddled her by pushing his hips into her curvy rump and pinning her down. Their sweat started to mix as Carlo's heavy breathing on her neck gave her tingles from head to toe.

'Really, Nicky...I no wants to hurt you...we finish now, OK?' he panted as he pressed his hips into her a little harder.

'You Soft Cock!' she yelled, as she wriggled under him.

Carlo, aroused by the position of his pelvis between her cheeks as well as their combined body heat, raised his hand and brought it down flush on her white fleshed buttocks: "SLAP!" Nicky nearly climaxed then and there and sucked in another few deep breaths before responding.

'Italian Faggot!' she said without conviction but hoping he'd get the hint.

Carlo wound up once more and slapped her on the butt again then — oh so gently — he leaned forward to nibble and suck on her ear, his hot breath giving her goose bumps on the back of her neck. He stopped after remembering that Tom was only a stone's throw away watching them.

'I take my shoes and I go now, OK? he whispered.

Nicky didn't answer straight away. She was still savouring the shudder she'd received from his last giddy-up slap.

'How about we go into my bedroom and we can finish off what we've started?' she finally purred.

Carlo had also reached the same conclusion!

He flipped Nicky over, picked her up in his arms, and carried her through the bedroom doorway and after stumbling over some of her lounge room furniture dumped her onto her bed with a squeal before diving in on top of her.

Across the street Tom nearly fell out of the tree trying to see what was going on through Nicky's bedroom window. After a moment it dawned on him that he'd just gone from being a witness to "All's Fair In Love And War" to actually being a "Peeping Tom." Deflated that his Italian flatmate was now enjoying the spoils of war he jumped out of the tree, hopped into his car, turned the ignition key, and put his foot flat to the floor spinning the wheels to fishtail for 20 metres before hitting the first turn and rounding out of Nicky's street.

Guessing the commotion outside was Tom's reaction to him bedding Nicky instead of their planned humiliation, Carlo decided it best to stretch the lust fest into a sleep over just in case his key no longer opened their front door.

CHAPTER XXII

SATURDAY was Alex's favourite day of the week. The morning usually started with a light breakfast at a trendy suburban café with her dad followed by a two hour Hip Hop dancing class at the grooviest dance studio in town. Then she either went for lunch with her fellow Groovers and respective mothers or back to one of their houses for an afternoon catch-up of teenage girly gossip, music, and boy talk.

However, today being the prelude to John's big romantic dinner date with Joan, it was to be strictly dad and daughter time. She'd talked him into buying a completely new outfit from top to toe, including new underwear and aftershave, as he was on a mission to irresistibly impress Joan.

John had resisted entering busy shopping malls at all costs for years but today it was all out of his control; Alex was in charge now and leading him by the hand like a lamb to the slaughter. The first items were the all important shirt and pants. They entered a trendy shop staffed by male and female assistants young enough to be Alex's older siblings. An assistant, Samantha, noticed them and offered the usual greeting.

'Hi there — are you looking for something in particular?'

'Yes, we're looking for the hottest men's outfit you have,' Alex responded, before John had a chance for an in.

Samantha had to hold her poise both towards Alex's response and John's shrug of communication to show that the entire situation was obviously out of his control.

'Certainly, madam. Please, follow me,' Samantha said, winking at John and letting him know she knew exactly how to play out the scene for maximum customer satisfaction. She led them to a rack of long-sleeved shirts. 'What size would Madam be interested in?'

Alex looked John up and down as a front to impressing Samantha but since they both alternated doing the washing at home she knew precisely both his shirt and pants sizes.

'Regular to Large,' Alex responded, then turned to inspect and feel the fabric of a few shirts. Alex took one, two, then three selections off the rack and handed them to Samantha. 'Now pants,' she announced, as she took John by the hand once again.

'This way please,' Samantha obliged with a hand gesture, a subservient bow, and a smile.

Alex took control in the same fashion and before Samantha could get a word of recommendation in she had two handfuls of shirts and pants ready for John to try. Samantha led John to the change rooms and put the selections on a hanger then directed John inside.

'Thank you very much, Samantha,' John said graciously before closing the door behind him.

Samantha rejoined Alex who was waiting near the change rooms like an expectant mother.

'So what's the big occasion?' Samantha asked.

'Don't tell anyone but dad's going on his big first date tonight,' Alex replied, excitedly.

'I see. He's a very lucky man to have a daughter who approves of him getting out there again,' Samantha smiled.

'I more than approve,' Alex stated with a cheeky grin: 'It was me who set them up!'

*****

A few suburbs away Carlo was doing the 'walk of shame' from Nicky's car to his front door loosely dressed in his alter ego Georgio's clothes from the night before. After waking up still tightly snuggled together he and Nicky had shared breakfast in bed followed by a little more feisty love making before collapsing exhausted into a late morning snooze.

Halfway down his front path Carlo turned around and blew Nicky a kiss goodbye. Nicky smiled at him before taking off, u-turning with a screech, then accelerating back past Carlo and Tom's house with a blast of her car horn. Still paranoid about the reception he'd receive from Tom, Carlo had asked Nicky not to make her exit so obvious, *But hey, that's Nicky,* he thought, always willing to perform the opposite of what had been asked.

Carlo closed the front door behind him hoping Tom was not home. The loud football commentary coming from the TV, however, confirmed there'd be no such luck. Two strides into the lounge he looked up to find Tom with his eyes glued to the TV. Without changing his line of sight, he addressed Carlo.

'So how was your date?'

'You see, I destroy her for you!' Carlo had no choice but to respond.

'Yeah, right. Exactly what did you destroy—her bed springs?' Tom retorted. It was a question too far above Carlo's level of English.

'Her what?' Carlo questioned.

'Nothing. Just forget it,' Tom replied, and turned the volume on the TV up even louder. Carlo retreated quickly to his bedroom, shut the door and crashed onto his bed. *Was last night with Nicky worth the $500 membership fee and this friction with Tom?* he questioned himself.

The answer shot back to him faster than a speeding bullet.

Damn right, Nicky rocks!

CHAPTER XXIII

WILL and Flea strolled the Mansion's opulent grounds together inspecting the final preparations for the night's Luv Inc singles shindig. Dozens of hired workers ranging from caterers, barmen, security people, professional decorators, and stage and lighting crews, to DJ Dr. YourTunes had from sunrise began to bump in. Now, just on sunset, most were tweaking or testing their equipment one last time.

Flea had personally handled a call from an anxious Ravi the day before: he had emphatically asked her to let him speak to Will but to no avail. As close as he could get to begging he implored Flea to cancel the night until after the first of next month so as not to affect the site's 30 day money back guarantee. This, however, was all she'd needed to hear and immediately after she'd hung up on him Flea rang her boss Randall to confirm the cracks were beginning to appear in the relationship wall between Will and Ravi. Over an expensive dinner Randall had clued Flea into his plan to use the party to decisively sink the Luv Inc ship once and for all. He'd even resolved to taking a personal hand to that effect by opting to be the official MC for the drawing of the lucky door prize, the brand new Alfa Romeo convertible.

Will and Flea walked into the middle of the marquee to inspect the dance floor. Once they reached the middle Will took Flea by the hand and swung her around for practice, like an aspiring Fred Astaire.

'It's going to be one hell of a party!' Will exclaimed, as Flea giggled.

'And by its end you'll be the King of the Internet Dating Tree!' she answered.

'How can I ever thank you?' Will asked.

'A promotion and a raise would be good,' Flea said in jest.

Will's answer was interrupted by applause causing him to look to a figure he didn't recognise standing nearby.

'Nice moves. You two make a good couple,' the stranger said.

'Hi Randy. Will this is Randy, our MC for the night,' Flea said as Randall shook Will's hand.

'I must say, Will, you got class,' Randall said as he squeezed Will's hand.

'I can't take all the credit—Flea's one hell of a PA,' Will replied taking his hand back.

'Don't I know it,' Randall replied. 'Do you mind if I borrow her for a few moments? I have a few things to go through to get us all in sync for tonight?'

'Sure, be my guest,' Will said. 'Actually I have to go home to get ready anyway so I'll see you back here at, say, eight?'

'It's a date,' Flea answered.

'Nice to meet you, Randy,' Will said.

'Likewise, Will. Catch you later!' Randall called, taking Flea by the arm and leading her to a more secluded spot. 'How're we looking?' he asked.

'At 10 Will draws the winner of the door prize; at 10:05 you make your announcements; at 10:10 all the members leave in disgust; at midnight Luv Inc is broke; and by 9am Monday we're ready for a takeover!'

'That's my girl,' smiled Randall, 'right down to the last detail.'

CHAPTER XXIV

RENE, Derrick, and Rene's mum, Kara, were sitting on the balcony of Rene and Derrick's penthouse apartment having a pre-dinner glass of Sauvignon Blanc and admiring an orange sunset over Mount Coot-tha. Kara felt a vibration in her handbag and retrieved her phone. She looked at the caller ID and noticed it was a blocked call. She came to the conclusion it couldn't be a direct marketing call, especially this time on a Saturday evening.

'This is Kara,' she answered.

On the other end of the line was Jane, one of People Power's most trusted babysitters. She was calling from a police station.

'Kara, I'm sorry, I can't come to work tonight,' she sobbed into the phone.

'Why? What's the matter, dear?' Kara inquired.

'I…I've been mugged… On the way to my car!' she cried.

'Are you OK? Is their anything I can do?'

'I've already rung my parents, there coming down to get me. The police need me to give them a statement and then I can go home,' she sniffed.

'Oh, sweety, I'm so sorry. Don't you worry, I'll find someone to take your shift. Don't feel obliged to come back to work till you're all in one piece again, OK?' Kara said.

'Thank you, Kara, thanks for understanding,' Jane said.

'You take care. And no, thank you, my dear,'

Kara confirmed.

'What's wrong?' Rene asked, noticing the concerned look on Kara's face.

'Poor young Jane's been mugged on the way to her job tonight,' Kara replied.

'How terrible,' Rene replied. 'Is she OK?'

'Fortunately yes. Unfortunately I have no-one left to replace her with,' Kara relayed.

'I'll do it!' Without hesitation Derrick offered his services.

Rene and Kara, whose relationship as mother and daughter often came with the power of knowing each other's exact thoughts at the same time, looked at each other with a knowing nod. Not wanting to damage his feelings, Rene came to the rescue.

'Nice offer, Derrick, but I think it best a People Power employee be the solution to this.' She turned to her mum. 'What's the name of the client and their address?' Rene asked as she put her glass down.

'John Trainer. You'll be taking care of his daughter, Alex. I can't recall the street but they live in Mount Gravatt,' Kara answered.

'Ah, yes, I remember taking that confirmation call from Celene,' Rene affirmed. She checked her watch and only then realised the urgency of the situation. 'Ring John and tell him I'm on my way. Text me their address when you get it — hopefully I'm not going to be too late!' Rene said, then dashed inside to change.

John was in the middle of modelling his new outfit for Alex, complete with shoes and a splash of his new aftershave, when his phone rang.

'Hello, this is John.'

'John this is Kara from People Power, the babysitting service for Luv Inc.'

'Yes, Kara, what can I do for you?' he asked as Alex circled him checking every detail.

'John I'm ringing to inform you that due to unusual circumstances your sitter is going to be a little late this evening.'

'How late?' he asked

'About 20 minutes. I can confirm she's already on her way, though,' Kara assured him.

'I see. Well not much we can do about it now, so we'll just have to be patient. Thank you for the call, Kara. Goodnight,'

'You're welcome, John. Good luck on your date,' Kara replied.

'So, what say you?' John looked to Alex for her critique on his outfit as he hung up.

'I picked it, remember?' she answered.

'OK, smarty,' he smiled.

'But your aftershave!' she went on, crinkling her nose. 'Joan doesn't stand a chance! Who was on the phone?' she asked.

'The dating company. Apparently the sitter's going to be a little late,' he answered.

'WHAT? After all we've been through to get tonight perfect the stupid sitter's going to be —'

'I'm nervous enough as it is Alex. They'll get here soon enough,' he assured her.

*****

134

After breaking the land speed record on the M1 highway Rene's GPS recommended taking exit 17 and going straight through the lights and up a hill. She took a left then a right at its apex then turned into John and Alex's street. She slowed to read house numbers and counted down from 32, 30, 28, 26 then pulled up outside number 24 Hill Street. Little did she know she was being spied on: Alex was watching for her arrival from an upstairs window.

'Dad the sitters here!' Alex cried out to John as she let the curtains fall closed.

John was in front of the bathroom mirror examining himself one last time. After checking his pockets for his keys and wallet he entered the lounge room to find Alex waiting for him wearing a painted Tahitian facemask to hide her birthmark. He knew there was no point making it an issue. He put his hand in his pocket and pulled out a $20 note and handed it to her.

'Here, just in case you get the munchies.'

'I love you, dad,' Alex said.

'I know,' John replied just as the doorbell rang. 'Wish me luck!'

'Break a leg,' she replied. They walked to the door together, opening it to a breathless Rene.

'Hi, I'm John and this is Alex,' he said, holding out his hand.

'I'm Rene, so nice to meet you both and I'm sorry about the delay,' she said, shaking his hand.

'I best get going,' John said, bending down to offer Alex a cheek to kiss and a shoulder to hug.

'Good luck — break a leg!' Rene said.

John and Alex looked to each other in recognition of the same salutation that Alex had also spoken seconds earlier.

'Thank you, Rene. You two have fun,' John said and walked to his car.

'So, where's *my* mask?' Rene questioned Alex playfully.

'Wanna listen to some music?' Alex countered.

'Thought you'd never ask,' Rene replied, and had Alex not been wearing her mask Rene would have witnessed the angelic smile underneath it that right now shone brighter than sunshine.

*****

John parked his car and quickly walked to Alberto's Italian restaurant. It was Joan's choice and one he'd never been to before but had heard on the grapevine that the food was divine.

'Can I help you, Signore?' the maître d asked him.

'I have a booking under "Trainer."'

'Ah, yes,' the maître d responded. 'La Signora is already here. I have already given her a drink,' he said, priming John for a big tip at the end of the night. 'Please follow me,' he offered.

John had butterflies in expectation of the first sight of Joan which erupted when he sighted an almost carbon copy profile of his deceased wife, Grace. Joan spotted him and stood up with a smile.

'Finally!' she said as he took her by the hands and looked deep into her crystal blue eyes.

'Finally!' he replied, as the maître d pulled back his chair and unfolded his napkin.

*****

At 22 Hill Street, Sally had to close her windows to shut out the party that was happening next door. The "BOOM BOOM" of Alex's favourite Hip Hop music would have given any residents within 100 metres of the house the same impression.

At 24 Hill Street the lounge, coffee table and floor mat had been moved out of the way leaving a perfectly polished wooden dance floor. Alex had learned many of the moves in the music clip in her Hip Hop class and was performing most of them on cue as Rene looked on applauding.

The track finished and led into another but Alex, who hadn't even broken into a sweat yet, glided to the TV remote and turned it down.

'You got some mojo there, girl!' Rene said in appreciation of the premium home entertainment.

'OK, now it's your turn!' Alex replied, evading Rene's praise.

'I don't do Hip Hop,' Rene said with a shrug.

'So what can you do?' Alex queried.

Rene put her hand out for Alex to pass her the TV remote. After catching it Rene began to surf through the music channels from 80s Retro to 90s Rock and beyond until she came to the aerobic/fitness station. To her delight she found a repeat episode from her favourite Zumba instructor from Latin America. She turned the volume up, threw the remote back to Alex, and began to whip up a Zumba storm to the exotic beats.

Halfway through the set Alex turned the volume down catching Rene by surprise.

'Wait, I've got a challenge!' Alex said.

'A what?' Rene replied

'Let's see whose got the best moves!' Alex challenged her excitedly.

Rene shook her head at her competitive nature. Besides, she wasn't dressed for dancing and her temperature was starting to rise.

'They're very different moves; besides, whose going to judge?' Rene countered.

Not one to be stopped in her tracks Alex picked up the phone and dialled, as Rene looked on oblivious.

'What are you doing?' Rene asked.

Alex pointed an index finger for Rene to wait a minute.

'I'd like to order two pizzas for home delivery please,' Alex said into the receiver. 'One large Hawaiian and one large Pepperoni. Thanks!' Alex hung up.

Shit. Rene couldn't remember the last time she'd seen, let alone eaten pizza, but she was somehow sure she was never going to forget tonight's treat.

*****

John passed a photo of Alex over the dinner table to Joan. They'd already ordered their entrées and were sipping their first glasses from a bottle of Chianti.

'She's so cute,' Joan observed, 'I'd love to meet her!' She was genuinely enthusiastic with her words and sentiments.

'I'm sure she feels the same way,' John replied.

'So you told her about me?' Joan enquired causing John to feel a little uncomfortable about how to answer.

'Every last detail,' he fibbed with a straight face and a secret smile.

*****

Tonight was 18-year-old Pete's first weekend shift delivering pizza. During his training his supervisor told him that under no circumstances was a driver to ever, ever enter a customer's residence. That rule was smashed when Rene, who in the interim had changed into some sexy gym clothes she'd left in her car, answered the front door, grabbed him by the hand, and led him upstairs. What happened next would perhaps elevate Pete into pizza delivery legend status!

Before he got a chance to ask for the pizza money Pete was blasted with a wall of sound and the performance of a masked, 4 foot tall Hip Hopper whose moves resembled those in a Beyoncé music video. As soon as Alex stopped dancing Pete couldn't help but put the pizza warmers down and join Rene in applauding the little starlet.

Rene then changed the TV channel to the Zumba station and began to bedazzle him with new rhythm and moves.

'Man, I love this funky Brazilian shit!' mused Pete, much to Alex's disdain…it was a contest after all!

When Rene finished Pete applauded again but was surprised with Alex's next query.

'So, who's got the best moves?' she demanded.

'Who…what?' Pete asked.

Rene did a little shimmy then asked again.

'You know, the best moves. We have a bet going and you're the judge. So, is it contestant A,' Rene pointed to Alex who took a bow, 'or contestant B?' She pointed to herself and curtsied.

Pete looked from side to side before he answered.

'How much is the bet?'

'20 bucks,' came Alex's quick reply.

'Ladies, I've never seen moves like those in a house before!' Digging into his moneybag Pete the

Pizza Boy pulled out their change then two $10 notes from his own wallet and handed one to each of them. 'Here — you both win!' he declared.

Alex jumped up onto a chair then she and Rene kissed Pete on either cheek.

'Thank you, Pizza Boy,' they said in unison.

'Damn I love working weekends!' Pete responded, then picked up his pizza warmers and made for the front door double time.

*****

John, who was now on his second glass of red wine, should have known better. He was a one glass screamer at the best of times but the truth be known he was actually really starting to like Joan and he was sure she liked him. However, Joan had been revealing some of the private content from the emails she and Alex had sent each other and he couldn't put up with answering her with half-baked lies anymore.

'Joan, I know this is going to be a little hard to fathom but it actually wasn't me who you've been sending emails to,' he sighed.

'What do you mean it wasn't you?' Joan questioned.

'You see, it was, Alex, my daughter. She took my credit card and a photo and put a profile of me up on Luv Inc without me knowing,' he finished, then flinched as he witnessed the expression on her face turn to rage.

'You mean I've been masterbat— talking to your teenage daughter these last two weeks?' she asked.

John nodded his head, the mood now sombre. Joan smirked, looked to the bottle of red wine on the table, picked it up, stood, then poured the remainder of the bottle over his head creating a splashing red waterfall. She slammed it onto the table and snatched her handbag.

'Looks like you don't get the girl this mission, 007,' she finished, and stormed out of Alberto's past a gob smacked maître-d.

*****

Alex and Rene were seated on the first floor veranda in the middle of laughing at something one of them had said when John's car pulled into the drive.

'Dad's home!' Alex said.

'Maybe he's not alone?' Rene said, causing Alex to look at her and share another giggle. They listened for two car doors to close and a female voice but it never came. He had surely arrived home solo.

John opened the front door and made his way upstairs smartly. From the lounge room he saw that the light from the veranda had formed Rene and Alex's silhouettes on the dividing curtain. He was in two minds about whether to change his clothes before seeing them but Alex made his mind up for him.

'Hi, daddy, we're out on the veranda,' she called.

John inhaled deeply, parted the curtain, and walked through the open glass doors to the veranda.

'Why are you home so early?' Alex asked.

As John came a little closer Alex of course observed the ugly red splash on his cream coloured shirt.

'What happened to your new shirt?' she asked, somewhat alarmed.

John noticed the pizza boxes on the table between them. He still hadn't eaten dinner and pointed to them, half starved.

'Give me a slice and I'll tell you all about it.'

In the hour or so since Pizza Boy Pete had left Alex had given Rene most of the family facts including the details of her late mother's unsuccessful battle with cancer. She'd also mentioned that her dad's date with Joan was her idea, although she left the credit card fraud out of that story. Rene felt empathy for the duo since she'd recently been through her own major trauma with her ex-fiancé and didn't want to intrude on their privacy any longer.

'I'll go, if that's OK,' she said to them.

'Please stay. Besides, you're never going to hear a story like this one again!' John replied.

'Maybe, but we have a story of our own to tell, don't we, Rene?' Alex said, not wanting to be out left out.

'OK, why don't you two tell your story first.'? John lifted the lid on the pizza box and grabbed a slice. He loaded a cold slice of pizza into his watering mouth and took a seat, ready for a story.

Rene and Alex looked at each other to decide who would start but the image of Pete the Pizza Boy standing in the lounge room dumbfounded while they performed for him made them both erupt into spontaneous laughter. John, delighted to hear his daughter had found her sense of humour once again, decided to break the deadlock.

'Well, Alex, it looks like you found the naughty twin sister you've always wanted!'

Alex looked up to her dad and saw a twinkle in his eye as he peeked at Rene and then back to her with a smile. She did the math and realised there was chemistry in the air. She approved.

'How about you start, Rene,' she said, 'I need a jacket.' Alex then made the move inside and left them alone.

'Actually before you start, Rene, tell me, didn't you arrive tonight in jeans and a sweater?' he questioned. 'What's with that gym outfit? Not that I really mind...' he grinned.

Rene couldn't help but laugh at his cheeky observation.

'How else could I win a dance off?' she asked.

'A dance off?' John questioned. 'OK, tell me from the beginning,' he said, knowing that with Alex almost anything extraordinary was possible.

It was an hour later that they realised Alex hadn't come back to join them. They went inside together to look for her and found her asleep on the lounge. Rene moved in closer and removed her mask. Her birthmark was one of the first topics Rene had asked him about after Alex had left their presence so it came as no surprise. It was followed by her assurance to him of what a great job he was doing as a single father. Rene stroked Alex's hair.

'Goodnight, sweet girl.'

'Thank you so much for tonight,' John said after leading Rene downstairs and to the front door.

'Please, it was totally all my pleasure,' she replied.

John wanted to kiss her before she departed. Had he known how much she also wanted that he would have led with his lips rather than with his right hand, which she warmly shook.

'Goodnight, Rene. Drive safe,' he said.

'I will. Goodnight,' she said, then turned away toward the street and her car.

John waited until she had pulled away from the curb to kick himself for not getting her number. He couldn't believe he'd never see or joke with her again.

Rene knew that offering her personal details to a client was a big no-no. Then she thumped the steering wheel in frustration: *Who could he complain to, mum's the boss!* She turned on her car stereo. As the music started to sooth her she remembered something that might be an excuse to get in touch with him again; but it meant that she'd have to go through Celene to keep it private.

CHAPTER XXV

CELENE had parked her car in the street that led to the Mansion at 7.45pm just in time to see Will arrive in a luxury taxi dressed in a suit jacket and jeans and smoking a cigar. In the past two hours she'd counted the arrival of another 300 female guests, some of whom were already well on their way to alcohol-induced bliss and all of whom were dressed like they were attending a bridesmaid convention.

The last guest to arrive pulled up in a late model Porsche parking two spots behind her. She watched in her rear-vision mirror as a circus ringmaster stepped out onto the road complete with top hat, walking stick, and manicured moustache. He was so focussed on the Mansion that he didn't notice Celene in her front seat as he swaggered past her car.

For Will the evening had been a game of cat and mouse. Every time he tried to get Flea's attention she would come up with a new excuse to leave his presence and attend to one problem or another. There were, however, a few legitimate problems, the most important being that their insatiable guests had drunk 40 cartons of champagne in the first hour and the caterer would not refill the fridges until Flea had Will sign a cheque for 50 more.

Flea spotted Randall near the DJ console and when their gaze met he pointed to his watch. She nodded her approval and looked around to find Will, who'd been cornered near the bar by 2 tanked forty-something's who were sizing him up for a ménage à trios.

'Excuse me, ladies, but I need the host of honour,' Flea said as she pulled Will from their clutches.

'Where are you going, Will?' one of them asked.

'It's time to draw the door prize,' Flea answered for him.

'You do still have your tickets don't you?' Flea asked, which made them shift their attention from Will to the new Alfa Romeo that was parked next to the dance floor and back to Flea. The taller of the two pulled her ticket from her bra.

'You better believe it sister,' she said, and held it up as proof.

Flea led Will by the hand through the crowd to join Randall at the DJ console. Randall smiled at Will then for the second time today gave him a cowboy-grip handshake.

'So, Will, you ready to become a star?'

'All the way, Randy!' he answered.

Randall let go of Will's hand and gave the signal to DJ Dr. YourTunes to fade the music down. Randall walked to the front of the stage with microphone in hand, much to the delight of the 300 strong female audience.

'Good evening, Luv Inc ladies, are you having a good time?' Randall announced like a Las Vegas boxing promoter.

The roar of applause and whistles of the now drunken crowd was deafening.

'Alright! Now's the moment you've all been waiting for — the drawing of the lucky door prize: a brand new Alfa Romeo convertible!' He paused to let the noise from the crowd die down a little. 'But first, please let me introduce to you the President of Luv Inc and our most generous host, Misterrrrr Williammmm JACKSONNNNN!' Again his words were rewarded with a rock star response.

Will walked onto the stage to join Randall.

'So, Will, how're you feeling about giving away this fine automobile?' Randall asked, angling the microphone for Will's response.

146

'To tell you the truth, I've never won anything in my life—I wouldn't mind winning it myself,' he answered honestly.

'I'm sure every guest here's feeling the same way so, ladies, can you please get your tickets out!' Randall asked.

He took a step toward a barrel that was near the DJ console and gave it a spin. When it finally stopped he gestured to Will to put his hand inside. Will retrieved a ticket and handed it to Randall.

'Alright! Can the holder of green ticket number 45 please come to the stage and collect your keys!'

The room fell silent. Some guests scrunched up their tickets and threw them to the floor in disappointment; others looked around for evidence of a winner. Finally Randall broke the stalemate.

'Don't be shy. Now come up and collect your keys,'

There was a movement at the back of the audience.

'I won! I won! I won!'

From their vantage point on the stage Will and Randall noticed the crowd start to part at the very back. Then a figure moved closer and closer to the stage until a small, frail woman, perhaps the oldest member of Luv Inc ran across the dance floor with a green ticket in her hand. She leapt onto the stage to maul Will, leaving lipstick all over his cheeks and nose, then snatched the keys from Randall after handing him the ticket.

'We have a winner! Congratulations on behalf of Luv Inc and staff,' Randall said. He signalled DJ Dr. YourTunes once more and this time the anthem Celebration by Kool And The Gang thumped the party into dance mode.

Flea nodded to Randall then stepped on stage to take Will by the hand.

'How about you and me go get some privacy?' she asked.

Will nodded and she quickly led him off the stage, across a grassy patch, and toward the back of the Mansion.

They rounded a corner and walked toward a blue-lit pool and spa. Flea led Will to a chair beside the pool then kicked off her shoes, tucked the bottom of her dress into her knickers, and took a seat at the pool's edge, immersing her legs in the refreshing water. The muted sounds of the party music seemed a thousand miles away as Will sat back to enjoy the crystalline reflections of the pool lights that played over Flea's face and bust.

'Can you believe that ancient granny won the Alfa? Talk about anticlimax,' he said.

'I know what you mean. It's like when you get this picture of events in your head then—BAM—something totally unexpected materialises,' she said.

'Wow, Flea, you like, so read my mind. OK if I join you?' he asked.

'Course not. You're the Prez after all,' she replied, and patted the tile next to her as an invitation.

Will pulled off his sneakers, stood and ripped off his jeans to unveil his favourite cartoon character boxer shorts, then took a seat by the pool next to her. The coolness of the water on his legs didn't stop the rush of blood he was feeling down below.

*****

Randall walked to the front of the stage microphone in hand. He signaled to DJ Dr. YourTunes and the music faded into silence. All eyes were glued to him as he brought the microphone to his lips.

'Ladies, can I have your attention please?' He looked around, savouring being the centre of Luv Inc.'s downfall.

'The reason for this party is because Luv Inc has some changes to announce. Due to economic stresses on the company all the member benefits will be cancelled from midnight tonight,' he announced, waiting for the information to sink in before continuing.

'We know that's hard to take, especially since you've all paid in advance and only just begun, but unfortunately there's not much we can do.' He paused once more for effect before continuing. 'Also, the bar is closed and we've run out of time for tonight, so I must ask that you please finish your drinks and leave as soon as possible. Thank you and goodbye,' he finished.

A murmur broke put coloured by many "BOOS" of disappointment. As if on cue, numerous security guards descended upon the crowd to help the ladies finish their drinks and escort them to the exit in record time.

Celene was out of her car and standing in the shadows not far from the entry gates. She'd heard every word of the announcement and although she'd resisted calling Ravi during the night this revelation was too great a bombshell to keep from him. She punched a button on her mobile to autodial him just as the first group of disappointed Luv Inc members started to exit the Mansion.

Poolside, Will stretched out a hand to touch Flea's naked thigh. Flea bitch-slapped his hand away.

'What do you think you're doing?' she screamed.

Will took no notice and moved in closer to kiss her. Flea used all her strength and pushed Will, jacket and all, into the pool. He came up for air looking like a drowned rat.

'What was that for?' he asked.

'I'm not that type of girl,' Flea responded, as if she was horrified.

'I'm sorry I just thought we had a connection. Isn't that why you brought me out here?' Will waded through the water toward the pool steps.

'Stop right there! One more move before I get out of here and I'm going to scream rape,' she threatened.

'OK, OK, calm down,' he said, watching helplessly as Flea took-off around a corner and out of sight.

Flea made her way through the marquee and joined Randall who was waiting for her just near the exit. They smiled at each other.

'From PA to Prez in two weeks — you should be proud,' he said, confident that the disgruntled Luv Inc punters they were trailing would pop Will and Ravi's bubble.

Randall took out his car keys and pressed the security button to open his Porsche. As Flea got to the passenger door both of them were startled by the bright flash of a camera. As Flea looked to see who was responsible, the culprit took a step backwards to hide behind a tree. Celene was annoyed that Ravi had not taken her call but was sure that her incoming text, which would include the photo she'd just taken, would get his attention.

Will put his jeans and sneakers on and made his way back to the marquee. He was flabbergasted that the lights had been turned on and that the staff were already busy packing up the whole shebang. Of most concern of course was where all his members had gone. He walked onto the stage and spoke to the DJ.

'Have you seen Flea?

'Yeah, she left about three minutes ago,' DJ Dr. YourTunes answered.

'Where did everyone go?' Will asked.

'The MC called the whole night off, something about the economic stress of Luv Inc. Shame,' he shook his head in disappointment,' I haven't even played my best records yet.'

Will jumped off the stage then a loud "BEEP BEEP" from the Alfa Romeo scared the shit out of him. Sitting in the driver's seat was the lucky door prize winner, now one of the only members left. Will waved to her, and the granny waved back at him and winked seductively.

'Hey, sonny. Need a lift?'

CHAPTER XXVI

CELENE was at home in front of her PC when Ravi finally called.

'What's going on?' he questioned.

'Have you checked the site?' Celene asked.

'No, why? What's the matter?'

'They've torpedoed Luv Inc—you're going down like a sinking ship.'

Ravi opened the laptop on the desk next to his bed and brought up the site.

'My goodness, we already have 100 requests for refunds,' he noted.

'They've started up a member blog as well. You need to shut the site down immediately,' she ordered.

'I can't,' Ravi said, 'I don't have all the access codes.'

'What! Who the hell has them, then?' Celene asked.

'It's a long story. I'm afraid we'll just have to go down with the ship,' Ravi surrendered.

'Ravi, I know who Flea really is and who she's working for: Who has the codes?' Celene asked again.

'The dean of my university, Mr. Chester.'

'Get them ASAP and I'll meet you for breakfast to discuss a counter attack,' she finished, then hung up.

Ravi's chatter had woken up his girlfriend who'd been sleeping next to him. The concept of Luv Inc was in fact hers from start to finish, an idea she'd come up with in bed just after she and Ravi first took their friendship to the next level. However, neither of them thought it would ever be taken seriously or actually convert to paying members.

The last few days had been ones of total frustration while she listened to Ravi's stories of the recklessness and arrogance of his business partner. On many occasions she'd wanted to handle the situation by confronting Will personally but there was simply too much at stake. If there was any hint that her relationship with Ravi was more than it should be they both knew it would give Will and his accomplice, Flea, the ammunition to sink them all.

'What's up, darling?' she asked.

'Trish, we need to talk to the dean,' he said.

'It's 12.30am. There's not much we can do now — come back to bed,' she suggested.

Ravi did as she asked and got under the covers, but Trish only pretended to go back to sleep. The cogs in her mind were turning as she contemplated Ravi's conversation with Celene and the deliberate nuking of Luv Inc by Flea. Trish now took these attacks on Ravi and their creation as a personal rebuke. She was recalling lines from her favourite tragedy "The Mourning Bride" which she'd studied in a classic English Literature class when she was in college long ago:

Yes, thou shalt know, spite of thy past Distress,
And all those Ills which thou so long hast mourned,
Heav'n has no Rage, like Love to Hatred turned,
Nor Hell a Fury, like a Woman scorned.

Trish Bain, Ravi and Celene met at a café for breakfast the next morning at 8.45. As they sipped their hot beverages Celene dived in with an intelligence report.

'A few years ago, I was at a marketing conference in Sydney. I remember at the celebration drinks on the last night I met an older man with his then young PA. We swapped cards, as you do at conferences, but I never heard from either of them again.'

'Where is this leading Celene?' Trish asked.

'I thought I finally remembered that day in Sachs office,' she said, 'but then when I saw her with him last night it all came back to me. I dug through my old files and I found these.' Celene put a hand into her pocket and pulled out two business cards and passed them to Ravi.

'Randall Stevens. CEO. Up2U.com,' he read out. 'What is that?' he asked.

'It's exactly what Luv Inc is — a dating site.'

'What a stupid name for a dating site,' Ravi responded, passing the card to Trish. 'And who is this person?' Ravi asked, looking at the other business card.

'That, my friend, is the card of his PA.'

'And why is it relevant?' he asked.

'Because today we know her as Flea!' she answered triumphantly.

'OK, I see why she's relevant, but what has Randall got to do with this?' Trish interjected.

'I'm glad you asked. It just so happens that Mr. Stevens was the MC for the party last night and it was he who made the announcements that sunk Luv Inc!' Celene said.

'So you think this whole episode is industrial sabotage?' Trish asked.

'I don't think so,' Celene said, 'I know so!'

Trish put a hand into her handbag and pulled out her phone.

'Who are you ringing?' Ravi asked.

'If what Celene is alleging is true it takes this to a whole other legal level and I have just the friend to help us when we get there!' she answered.

'What about the access codes, Trish?' Ravi questioned. Trish patted him on the arm and smiled.

'That, my dear, is my next call.'

CHAPTER XXVII

THE last thing Chester needed to add to his conscience was breaking his word to his priest. He knew the upcoming turnoff was where Laura would figure out that they were not on course to visit his sister; he was, however, en route to keeping his promise to Father O'Leary. Chester steered straight ahead and didn't make the turn.

'Where are we going?' she asked.

'Someplace we haven't been to for way too long,' he replied.

'What do mean? Turn back—you can't keep Silvia waiting,' she said.

'She's not waiting...I made that up.'

'You mean you lied?' Laura retorted.

'In all the years we've been together have I ever lied to you?' he asked. He didn't get a response but Laura's contemptuous stare, which he observed via the rear-vision mirror, was deafening.

Chester slowed down as they drove over the hill leading into Samford Valley: these were the fields in and around which he and Laura had grown up. He took a right past his old primary school and then a quick left into the car park of a picnic ground before stopping. He pressed the button for the van's rear elevator door to open.

Had his phone, which was connected to the dashboard, not been on silent he would have heard Trish Bain's call but today he had just one focus: *"Try and rekindle your first love."* These words from Father O'Leary had continued to echo in Chester's head from the moment he spoke them during his confession.

As Laura eased herself down via the rear elevator Chester retrieved a picnic hamper and blanket off the front seat. He closed the door and heard the crunching of Laura's wheelchair as it rolled over the loose stones of the car park. He continued down a short path that led to a clearing dominated by a 30 metre tall Ghost Gum. He spread the blanket and put the picnic basket down, turning to Laura who'd caught up with him. He motioned for her to follow him behind the tree.

Once on the other side of the tree he stopped and looked up. *I'm so glad you can still see it,* he thought. What Chester had spotted was the initials LM/LC inside a love heart carved deep into the trunk. He'd inscribed it with his pocketknife over 40 years ago; it was higher now than it had seemed before. He pointed to it as Laura wheeled to a spot beside him and looked up.

'We made love that night remember?' he recalled. 'Right here, on a blanket under the stars.'

'That was a long time ago when I was young and beautiful,' she said. ' I'm not that woman anymore.'

'I proposed here, Laura, and you didn't hesitate to say yes. You need to know that I've always kept my vows to you!' he pleaded.

Laura turned her wheelchair in the other direction.

'Perhaps you shouldn't have.'

Back at their local church in Brisbane Father O'Leary was kneeling in front of the altar praying for Chester and Laura, beseeching the Almighty for a miracle. He rose to his feet and after crossing himself he lit a candle and put it into a holder. He felt confident that someone of Chester's character and devotion deserved to have a supplication on his behalf answered. He remembered the day he'd decided to enter the priesthood and the vow of celibacy that went with the office.

'Thy will be done, on earth, as it is in heaven,' he quoted, before bowing before the alter one last time, accepting the situation was now out of his hands, and totally in the control of his creator.

*****

The sunburnt bark of a Ghost Gum is the perfect camouflage for the Eastern Brown Snake, the second deadliest land serpent on earth, so Laura had no clue that she'd just run over the tail of one of the two metre long creatures. The snake is also recognised as being the most aggressive in Australia: in a flash it reared up, baring its fangs, and latched onto Laura's bare leg, injecting enough venom into her to kill a dozen men. Her scream was more out of shock than pain due to her existing paralysis. Chester came around the tree just in time to see the snake slither away.

'LAURA!' he yelled, and scrabbled to her side.

'It bit me, on my left leg,' she answered.

'Darling, hold on. I'll get you to a hospital.' Chester took the handles of her wheelchair and pushed her toward the path leaving his blanket and picnic basket behind. They dashed into the car park; he was desperately looking for his car keys while at the same time trying to keep her chair moving forward. 'Hold on, we're nearly there.'

Chester hit the release button for the van's wheelchair elevator to unlock. It opened and he let go of Laura's chair, took hold of the elevator from the top lip, and used all of his body weight to help pull it down. He pushed Laura inside and strapped her in. He jumped out of the van, pushed the button for the rear door to secure, then helped the elevator door close before rushing to the driver's door and jumping inside.

'We'll get there darling. Stay strong for me,' he pleaded.

'I'm feeling faint, Lorrie. Please…please hurry,' she said, already out of breath.

Chester exited the car park and hit the road with speed. He looked back in the rear-vision mirror and noticed Laura shaking and blinking uncontrollably. He'd seen her in this helpless state once before when she'd come off her horse and been crushed by its weight. He wept, knowing that the venom from a brown snake could kill in less than 20 minutes if untreated. He reached for his mobile and dialled 000.

'Emergency services, how may I direct your call?' a female voice asked.

'I need medical assistance — my wife's been bitten by a brown snake. We're travelling toward Brisbane via Samford and we need to get to the closest open hospital with anti-venom,' he said with urgency.

'Stay on the line, Sir, we'll direct you there and prepare them for your arrival.'

20 minutes later Chester pulled up at the emergency section of Northside Medical with a now unconscious Laura in the back. Waiting expectantly for them were Dr. Roberts and two senior male nurses.

Not wanting to wait for the rear elevator to come down to unload her the nurses opened the van's side door, leapt inside, then carefully unloaded a motionless Laura onto a mobile bed.

'Are you sure it was a brown snake?' Dr. Roberts questioned Chester, shining a light into Laura's eyes.

'Positively,' he said, 'I've seen dozens of them growing up.'

'That information may well be her saviour,' the doctor responded.

Chester followed the trio as they rushed her through the automatic doors and into an emergency treatment station. A female nurse carrying a clipboard took Chester by the arm as Dr. Roberts issued instructions for the anti-venom injection.

'Mr Chester, could you please follow me?' she asked.

'Of course,' he said. 'Take good care of her, she's all I have left,' he said to the team working desperately on Laura to save her life.

Chester turned away from them just as one of the male nurses shook his head informing Dr Roberts that Laura didn't have a pulse. The doctor responded by pulling round the curtains for privacy as the nurses cut Laura's blouse from her body.

'I need you to fill out these forms for our records,' the nurse said to Chester. 'Also, we have to know if your wife is allergic to any medication, as well as her general medical history.'

'Yes, yes, of course,' Chester answered absently.

The nurse led Chester towards the reception area when he noticed a sign with an arrow pointing to the Chapel. Chester took the clipboard and pen from the nurse.

'Do you mind if I do this in there?' he pointed to the sign.

'Of course not, just bring it back as soon as you're done,' she responded.

'Thank you.' Chester turned a corner and then entered the chapel. It was lit dimly by an electric Dove of Peace leadlight. He walked past three rows of chairs, put the clipboard and pen on a front row seat, and fell to his knees in distress.

*****

'Clear!' called Dr. Roberts. He attached the two metal paddles of the defibrillator to each side of Laura's chest then pressed a button that injected 500 volts of electricity into her lifeless body. Her torso jumped inches off the bed then came back down with a thud. All eyes were fixed on the electrocardiogram for a reading. It flatlined.

Dr. Roberts increased the dose to 750 volts and waited for the red light to confirm the defibrillator was good to go again.

'Clear!' he called and applied the paddles to Laura's chest in the same manner as before. Laura's body reacted with a jump but the electrocardiogram again showed the flatline of a lifeless body. He then switched the defibrillator to 1000 volts, knowing that this was the last gamble he could take on a woman of Laura's age and condition. The red light came on and his staff stood back as he applied the metal paddles to her chest one last time.

'Clear!'

In the chapel Chester was still on his knees, first sobbing, then begging, and finally confessing. He couldn't take it anymore.

'I should be the one taken first! It was me who was weak! I beg you — PLEASE — let Laura live!'

CHAPTER XXVIII

AFTER spending another energetic night together, Nicky and Carlo used Sunday morning to put Nicky's apartment furniture back in place. Afterwards, Carlo wanted to take her out for brunch but she asked for some alone time to sort her emotions and feelings out.

After Carlo had left, Nicky went for a walk through a nearby park and past a children's playground. The sight of young parents playing with their children, cooking BBQ's, and laughing together had stirred her maternal instincts to boiling point.

She arrived back home resolute. She went through her bedroom and bathroom with a small box in hand and packed into it all the items that belonged to Kate: toiletries, spare clothes, underwear, and the photos of them together. Then, box in hand, she jumped into her car on a mission.

She arrived at Kate's apartment unannounced but was still well received and invited inside for a drink, which she declined. Instead, she handed Kate the box.

'Can we still be friends?' she asked, hopeful that she could remain on good terms with her Sensei, especially since the national championship was only a week away.

Kate didn't answer, but invited her inside once again, and once again Nicky resisted, knowing that it would lead to her 'fessing up about Carlo. She left Kate standing in her doorway, box in hand and sensing their relationship had all but dissolved.

*****

162

Trish, Ravi and Celene had once again met at a café, but this time they had been joined by an old friend of Trish's, Detective Barney Steel. They were huddled around Ravi's laptop while Ravi went through Luv Inc.'s 200—and rising—member refund requests that were linked and supported by dozens of defamatory member blog comments.

Detective Steel had already made some notes when Celene gave him details regarding the boardroom meeting and the events of the Luv Inc Mansion party. Ravi looked at Barney.

'What do you think, Detective Steel?'

'It doesn't look very promising, to be honest.'

'Why so, Sir?' Ravi asked.

'The main problem is that Will had employed all these people to represent the company,' he replied. 'It's going to be very difficult to prove that they weren't acting on his advice. It is a free country after all.'

'Could you try calling the dean again?' Ravi asked Trish.

'Sure thing,' Trish replied, and picked up her phone.

'Ravi, I have some ideas that may help, but the answers to them are not in my field of expertise,' Steel offered. 'Let me get in contact with an associate, get some particulars, and in a day or two I might have something.'

'With all due respect, Detective, I'm afraid that in a day or two Luv Inc is going to be business history!' Ravi replied.

Trish watched Ravi as she was listening to her phone and shook her head as she only got through to voicemail. Detective Steel noticed Ravi's disappointment.

'Look, no promises on a Sunday, but I'll break the rules and try my contact at home,' Steel said.

He took out his phone and dialled the home number of Detective James Kerrin, head of the police Information Technology Fraud and Computer Related Crimes task force. If anyone could find a trespass within industrial law he was your man. Detective Steel was doubly fortunate: not only was Kerrin at home and answering his call but, he recalled, Kerrin was indebted to him for a big favour from a long, long time ago.

CHAPTER XXIX

WITHIN the dimly lit chapel Chester had lost all sense of time. He was lying prostrate on the floor, his eyes closed, when the nurse entered.

'Mr. Chester, are you OK?' Startled, he lifted his torso off the floor and turned to face her.

'Yes. How is Laura?' he asked.

'Dr. Roberts has asked to speak to you privately,' she replied in a sombre tone. 'Please follow me.'

Chester sprang to his feet and followed her down a corridor to a private part of the hospital. She came to a door and knocked softly.

'Come in.' The nurse opened the door into a small office where Dr. Roberts was seated consulting a medical journal. He stood up when Chester entered.

'Where's Laura? Is she OK?' Chester whimpered.

'Mr. Chester, before I let you into the next room I have to prepare you.'

'My God, is she alive?' Chester asked in horror.

Dr. Roberts looked to the nurse who put a comforting hand onto Chester's shoulder.

'Sir, years ago, in a medical journal, I read of a very similar case to what's happened to your wife. Now, even though I've seen it with my own eyes, I'm still astounded,' he said.

'Is she alive?' Chester asked again, this time louder.

'Please, take a look for yourself,' Dr Roberts offered, opening up the other door in the room that Chester had not noticed when he had first walked in.

Chester slowly walked into the room and looked inside: his eyes bulged and his chin dropped to the floor. Laura was standing-up unaided next to a window taking in the view.

'My darling!' she said happily, turning to face him.

Chester stumbled and had to use the door handle to catch his fall. Laura opened her arms inviting him to come to her.

'I...I don't believe it...where...?' he rushed into her arms and held her tight.

'The venom from the snake has worked as an antidote to her paralysis,' Dr Roberts explained. 'The odds of that happening are perhaps half a billion to one.'

Laura kissed Chester repeatedly on the face then held his cheeks in her hands.

'You brilliant man! You dear, loving, brilliant man,' she said.

'Brilliant? What did I do?' he asked.

'What? You took me to see our tree, and look! Look darling, I'm free again!' she said, kissing his forehead. 'Can you ever forgive me?' she asked.

'Forgive you?' Chester questioned as he began to shed tears of delight, guilt, and relief.

'I've been terrible and nasty to you for all these years, and you...you've never left my side. Please forgive me?' she begged him, pressing him into her chest, her tears spilling onto him.

'In sickness and in health, remember?' he answered.

Dr. Roberts backed out of the room.

'What's your recommendation, doctor?' the nurse asked, still standing in the doctor's office watching the two lovers.

'Best to keep her in for observation overnight, just in case. If she's still walking in the morning then I think we've just witnessed a double miracle.'

CHAPTER XXX

MONDAYS were always busy at Up2U.com but this morning it was frantic. Wanting to capitalise on Luv Inc.'s weekend misfortune, Randall ordered the marketing staff to send direct emails to all their former clients who had joined LuvInc.com, urging them to reactivate their Up2U.com accounts. Randall also wanted to personally congratulate Hacker with his promised pay rise and promotion. He entered Hacker's workstation and slapping him on the back.

'I think its time we got you out of this cubicle and into a real office,' Randall said.

'Thank you, Boss,' Hacker replied, relieved he didn't need to remind him.

Detective James Kerrin had, in the meantime, pulled up in the Up2U.com car park with two other unmarked police cars. Five other young detectives followed him into the foyer where he flashed his badge and a warrant to the flustered receptionist. After getting instructions from her they filed past and through the doors that led into the main office.

Randall looked up to see them heading straight for him. Kerrin led his men directly to Hacker's workstation but Randall put in the first word.

'Can I help you?' he offered, standing his ground.

'I'll get to you in a second,' Kerrin barked. He turned to face Hacker. 'Are you Françoise Acolyte?' he asked a stunned Hacker.

'Oui,' he said in his native tongue.

'We have a warrant for your arrest and to seize your computer and hardware. Stand up,' he ordered.

'What am I under arrest for?' Hacker stuttered, looking firstly to Randall for help, then back to Detective Kerrin.

'Computer hacking, stealing and being an accessory after the fact,' Kerrin stated, as one of the young detectives slapped handcuffs over his wrists and took him away. Two other detectives then entered his workstation and began to shutdown and disassemble his computer.

'Are you Randall Anthony Stevens?' Kerrin then turned to address the now nervous CEO.

'Yes...I am,' was his reluctant reply.

'We have a warrant to search your workplace—do you have anything you want to declare before we do that?' Kerrin presented Randall with some paperwork as he asked his question.

Randall shook his head.

'OK, we'll do it the hard way. Can you take us to your office?' Kerrin asserted.

As Randall led Kerrin and his crew away he sensed every eye in the office was trained on him.

*****

In the president's office, Flea had just finished going over the details of her contract with Will. The Luv Inc contract contained a clause that included Abigail as part of the office fixtures and fittings: it truly was a deal with legs!

'Sign here, date there, I'll witness it, and we're all done,' she said, matter-of-factly.

'Flea, I think it best I talk to Ravi before I sign anything,' he said. 'And I'm not real sure I want to part with Abigail just yet.'

'Will, you've seen the 250 requests for refunds with your own eyes: that's $125,000 in cash. Do you have that kind of money?' Flea asked

'Not after the party,' he confirmed.

'Well, if you don't sign right here, right now, I'm leaving, and this deal comes with me.'

Their heads turned with lightning synchronicity as Detective Steel strolled boldly into Will's office with a bundle of paperwork in his hands. He flashed his police badge that sat on his belt as three rookie detectives also filed into the room behind him.

'Detective Steel CIB. Are you Gloria May Olsen?' he asked a gobsmacked Flea.

'Her name is Felicity Rea—' Will tried to answer for her but was cut off by detective Steel.

'Shut-up dickhead, I'm not talking to you,' he spoke to Will while facing Flea. 'One last time: Miss, are you—'

'Yes I am,' Flea interrupted, not wanting to hear that horrible name of hers again.

'This is a warrant for your arrest,' Detective Steel said as two of the rookie cops lifted her to her feet, cuffed her, and unceremoniously took her away.

Steel reached behind his back, took hold of his handcuffs from the leather pocket on his belt, and put them on Will's desk. As Will looked up from his seated position to the intimidating 6'3 career cop he was close to bursting his bladder onto the floor below. Detective Steel read the gold president's plaque in front of him then retrained his line of sight onto Will.

'William Jackson I presume?'

*****

Central Police Station's interview section is the largest, state of the art facility of its kind in Brisbane. Running parallel to the three side-by-side rooms, which all contained a small desk and three chairs, was an observation area with one-way glass panels on the wall so senior officers and technicians could observe and record the interviews in progress.

Trish, Ravi and Luv Inc.'s lawyer Fred Gower had been allowed special access into the observation section by Detectives Kerrin and Steel so they could witness the interrogations. In Room One, two rookie detectives were interrogating Hacker. In the middle room Gloria Olsen, AKA Flea Reardon, was seated facing an older male detective. The last room contained Will who was by himself and pacing like a caged tiger.

'Why hasn't Randy been arrested yet?' Ravi asked Detective Kerrin.

'We don't have enough evidence yet, but you never know what information people give up under interrogation,' he advised. He turned the volume switch up on Room Two. They could hear both Flea and her interviewer's voice as clear as a bell.

'So, you're willing to make a statement against Mr. Stevens?' the detective asked.

Before answering Flea undid the top button of her blouse.

'If you drop the charges there could be more,' she offered seductively.

Kerrin turned the volume back down then pointed to Hacker.

'The computer techs upstairs tell me this guy's hacked into enough databases to solve the mysteries of the universe,' he said with a chuckle.

'Why is Will under arrest?' Concerned about Will's obvious anxiety, Trish offered a question of her own.

Steel coughed then scratched the back of his head in bewilderment.

'Funny thing, that. I was in his office and put my handcuffs on his desk to adjust my pants. I read his name from the plaque on his desk and then he picked them up and cuffed himself. So, officially, he's not!' he said, laughing. 'But I'm sure we're going to get something on him.'

Fred Gower waved Trish and Ravi to the back of the room for a conference. He pointed to Will through the one-way glass as he whispered his advice to them. Eventually they came to an agreement and all shook hands. Gower took a few steps towards Detective Steel.

'How long can you keep him in there without laying any charges?' he asked.

'Maximum four hours,' Detective Steel replied.

Gower turned to Trish and Ravi and gave a thumbs-up. Then he turned back to the detective.

'That will do nicely,' Gower confirmed, then motioned for the duo to join him outside.

In the hallway Trish and Ravi listened intently as Gower gave strict instructions to his PA via his phone.

'Make three copies and have Simon bring them all to me down here before one o'clock,' he ordered before hanging up.

At five past one Detective Steel burst into Will's room, slammed the door behind him, slapped a bundle of papers onto the table, then pointed to a shocked William Jackson.

'You're looking at some serious jail time my young crook!' he barked before skimming a chair across the room and into the wall.

'Wha...what have I done?' Will questioned.

'I ask the questions in here, pal.' Detective Steel picked up the bundle of papers from the table and pretended to read from them. 'Fraud, tax evasion, false advertising... It's all here – in black and white – and indisputable!' he said, holding the papers inches from Will's face.

'I want my lawyer,' Will whimpered.

'Can't take the heat, can you, tough guy?' the detective mocked.

Will wiped a bead of sweat from his forehead.

'We thought as much,' Detective Steel said, then without warning he turned and exited the room, papers in hand.

As Trish and Ravi continued to witness the spectacle through the one-way glass Fred Gower entered the room holding his thick lawyer's briefcase, much to Will's relief.

'Fred! Thank God you're here,' Will said, taking hold of his pistol hand to shake it.

'You're in deep, Will, but I made a deal for you,' he said before placing his briefcase on the table and taking a seat.

'What have they got?' Will questioned.

'What? They have everything, including a statement from Flea who's confessed to the whole scheme,' he replied.

'What scheme?' Will asked.

Fred dug into his briefcase and took out some papers in triplicate, putting them on the table in front of Will.

'Do you want to get out of here?' he asked.

'Of course,' Will replied.

'Then all you have to do is sign these and I guarantee you that you're home free. Today,' Fred assured him. He unclasped a gold fountain pen from his shirt pocket and offered it to him.

'Shouldn't I read these first?' Will asked.

Fred snatched his pen from Will's grip and then took the papers from the table and stuffed them back into his briefcase.

'What are you doing?' Will asked.

'Son, I've just used the last favour I'm owed from my inside source to put this deal together. If you can't appreciate that then I'm out the door!' he said.

'OK, OK, I'll sign it! Just get me out of here!' Will said.

Fred put the contracts back onto the table in front of Will and offered his fountain pen once again. As he put his head down to sign the papers, Fred gazed sneakily at the one-way glass and gave Ravi and Trish a cheeky wink.

CHAPTER XXXI

EVER since leaving the hospital Chester and Laura felt like part of a travelling sideshow when presenting walking Laura to the world. So overwhelming was the proof before their eyes that Chester had decided to take a week off work to soak up the jubilation.

It was also a fantasy come true for Chester to chauffer Laura around in his red MG convertible once again. The car was parked next to the training paddock as he and Laura watched her favourite horse and rider make their way toward the last three hurdles,

'Watch this,' Laura said: Penny cleared the first, second, and third set with ease. 'Brilliant!' Laura cried out, as Penny and the horse made their way back around to join them.

'Thank you, Laura,' Penny said with pride.

'No, thank you, Penny, for being the best student in my world,' she replied.

Penny rode off to stall her stallion leaving Chester and Laura alone.

'Your chariot awaits, my lady,' Chester said.

Laura held out her hand for the keys.

'My gosh, this is a first!' Chester said, passing Laura the keys to the MG.

Laura made her way to the driver's side, jumped in, and started up the red rocket. Chester took his place next to her in the passenger seat.

'For 10 years I've been practicing in a wheelchair,' she said, then leaned over and gave Chester a kiss on the cheek. 'Now I'll show you what this baby can really do!' she said, pushing the accelerator to the floor, spinning the wheels, and speeding off over the hills.

CHAPTER XXXII

WILL was at home when he received a call from Ravi informing him that he was passing by and wanting to pick up the keys for the Luv Inc office. He'd spent the last few days wondering how Ravi had managed to get them out of the company without going bankrupt and finally ended up putting it all down to Ravi's obvious business genius. He was also stoked with his first ever top-of-the-class grade for a project, and with the memory of being *the* man — even if it was for just one night — of a first class Mansion party.

Will exited his apartment and made his way downstairs to find Ravi on the sidewalk waiting for him. He approached with a smile and an outstretched hand.

'Hey, Ravi, I just want to say sorry for blowing Luv Inc, man,' he said, passing the office keys to his former partner before they shook hands.

'William, it was just an exam. Besides, my family back home in Pakistan would never understand me owning that type of business,' he said.

'So, where are you off to now?' Will asked

'The same place you should be — on vacation,' Ravi answered. 'Which reminds me,' Ravi said, before walking back towards a car parked on the road. Will looked into the front seat, recognising the driver, while Ravi opened the back door and dug around for something. He returned with a package in his hands that he passed to Will.

'Ryan Davis?' Will questioned, looking at the addressee.

'I wanted to send it from New Zealand but perhaps a personal delivery will rub extra salt into his wounds,' Ravi replied.

'Man, I totally forgot about all that!' Will laughed, pulling Ravi closer to him.

'Ravi, what's going on with you and Trish Bain?' he asked in a whisper.

This time Ravi's memory was jogged.

'William, remember the night I promised to tell you how I knew to build the site before we got the exam papers?' he asked. 'Well, there's your answer!' he confirmed.

'Man...' It took a moment for Will to comprehend the situation. 'We could have been EXPELLED FOR THAT SHIT!' he blurted out.

'Shhhhhhhhhh,' Ravi said, putting an index finger to Will's lips, 'that's our little secret now.' Ravi slapped Will on the back and jumped into the passenger seat.

As Ravi and Trish took off Ravi stuck his hand out of the window to wave goodbye and Trish beeped the horn. Will waved back to them and smiled. *It's nice to know I'm not the only toy-boy round here!*

*****

The new President of Luv Inc had spent the morning settling into her new office. Most of the afternoon had been spent on the phone personally reassuring every member she contacted that not one Luv Inc benefit had been removed. In fact, Celene had been so busy that she'd forgotten about lunch. She was standing next to Abigail's tank with her phone headset on, finishing up her conversation with a member, when her stomach started to growl.

'Thank you, again, for your understanding and patience during this most difficult period. Goodbye.' Celene looked at Abigail: *What the hell do tarantulas eat?* She opened a few cupboards looking for a pet food container, or something, anything that might give her a clue as to Abigail's recommended diet. Then she realised the obvious: *If a dingbat like Will could keep a spider alive, surely anyone could!*

CHAPTER XXXIII

NICKY was feeling the pain of the blows she'd received during all the bouts leading up to the Australian Karate Championship final. Although it was being held in her hometown of Brisbane she hadn't seen her former Sensei, Kate, in the crowd, which dealt her a slight moral blow. She had to focus, block it all out of her mind, as her nemesis, three time Australian Champion Olivia Carter, shaped up to her again. This contest is what she had trained for, and it had been one damn long and hard year. It was also the reason she'd joined Luv Inc—to learn how to outwit Olivia with a new fighting technique.

Nicky was 2-1 ahead on points: the first to three points would get the trophy. She had to go for it. Just one more point and it was all hers. Nicky advanced toward Olivia, dummied a kick, then spun round with an outstretched arm, but her opponent was ready for the move: she blocked the arm then snuck a punch into her kidneys. Nicky went down onto the mat in pain. The referee raised a green flag.

'Point to Olivia Carter: the score is 2-2,' he confirmed. 'The next point will decide the Australian Championship!'

'Come on, Nicky, you can do it!' Nicky's hometown crowd really lifted their cheers for her. 'Nicky! Nicky! Nicky!' they chanted.

Nicky snap-sprang to her feet and the referee had the two opponents face off and bow to each other in respect in the centre of the ring. When Nicky came up she saw her new karate mentor, Carlo, seated in the grandstand above Olivia's head. He had a cap on, backwards like a baseball catcher, and signalled a move to Nicky. She shaped up to Olivia again then dummied a punch, one, two, three kicks and "BULLSEYE!" she hit Olivia with an actual punch to the heart. The referee's flag went up and the black belt master grabbed Nicky by the hand.

'Winner and new Australian Karate Champion—Nicky Kross!' he announced.

The home crowd jumped to their feet clapping and screaming in delight. Nicky jumped for joy, fists clenched and punching the air, before reaching out and shaking Olivia's hand.

'Great match, Nicky. You deserved to win,' said the gracious defending champion.

'Thanks, O, you're one tough bitch to beat!' Nicky replied. She noticed that Carlo was now standing only a few metres from the mat, smiling and clapping his champion dynamo of a girlfriend. She couldn't wait until after the trophy presentation and ran to him, diving into his arms. She kissed his cheek and neck as he held her in his arms.

'You are winner, Miss Tricky Nicky!' he said, teasing.

'That's right Mr. Looking4Kicks—I'm bad and I know it!' she said then slapped him playfully on the cheek.

Carlo kissed her once more and finally let go of her so she could return to the mat to receive the champion's trophy and savour the rapturous applause of her delighted local supporters.

CHAPTER XXXIV

RENE swung her handbag over her shoulder before switching off People Power's office lights. It had been a long, busy day, and she was hungry and overtired. One of the day's highlights, however, had been the news that Celene was now the president of Luv Inc. She'd waited a few days before touching base with her to confirm if the feelings and thoughts she had for John were the real deal: Affirmative!

She closed then locked the front doors and turned towards the street where she stopped, frozen solid in her tracks. Standing next to a traffic sign holding a paper shopping bag in one hand and Alex's hand in the other was the man she'd been thinking about for days. As she approached them, John held out the shopping bag for her.

'I thought you might be wanting these,' he said, as she took it from his grip.

Rene had a feeling she knew what was inside which was confirmed when she had a peek and spotted the sweater and jeans she'd left in their spare bedroom after her costume change and the unforgettable dance-off.

'You could have mailed them, you know,' she said, trying to play hard to get.

'I washed them for you but it was dad's idea to bring them back,' Alex stated.

'Is that a fact?' Rene asked, then she and John shared a knowing smile. 'I'm starved,' Rene said. 'How about we all share some pizza to celebrate the return of my gear?'

'Never thought you'd ask,' came Alex's flash reply.

Rene took John by the hand and they all started to walk.

'Dad said he thinks you left them on purpose so you could come back to get them,' Alex said.

'Alex, please,' John said, now embarrassed to the max.

'Did he now?' Rene replied, overjoyed that he felt the same way as she did.

'So?' Alex asked her.

'So what?' Rene asked her back.

'Did you leave them on purpose so you could come back to see us again?' Alex asked.

Now it was Rene's turn to feel embarrassed. She chose her response carefully.

'Umm...not telling,' she said with a laugh.

As they approached a telephone booth Alex broke away from them and put a finger into the coin return, getting lucky and retrieving a gold coin.

'Look!' she said, and held it up for them to see. 'Heads you did leave them on purpose, tails you didn't,' she said, flipping the coin into the air and catching it before slapping it onto the back of her wrist. 'Ready?' she asked.

John and Rene were now caught up in her playfulness.

'Ready,' Rene replied.

Alex lifted her hand oh so slightly to see the coin. Just as John and Rene moved closer to take a peek, Alex, quick as a flash, whisked it into her pocket.

'So what was it?' Rene asked.

'Not telling,' Alex replied.

'Come on, Alex, that's not fair,' John said.

'You don't really want to know,' Alex said with finality.

She ran ahead of them and stopped. She turned suddenly to face them, pointing to each of them in turn as she sang.

'Rene and Johnny, Sittin' in a tree:

K–I–S–S–I–N–G!'

THE END

ABOUT THE AUTHOR

Tonino's writing career began as a staff journalist with Australia's first E-Zine publisher in 2002. In 2006 he began writing feature scripts and after attaining his film producer's credentials in 2011, he commenced his own multi-media production company. Internet Dating Four Dummies was his fourth script and the first work he's adapted into a novel. He lives in Brisney Land & is often visited by a wild kookaburra.

www.ingramcontent.com/pod-product-compliance
Lightning Source LLC
Chambersburg PA
CBHW050941120626
46552CB00001B/319